STUMBLING
into LOVE

OTHER BOOKS BY AURORA ROSE REYNOLDS

The Until Series

Until November
Until Trevor
Until Lilly
Until Nico
Second Chance Holiday

Underground Kings Series

Assumption
Obligation
Distraction

Until Her Series

Until July
Until June
Until Ashlyn

Until Him Series

Until Jax
Until Sage

Shooting Stars Series

Fighting to Breathe
Wide Open Spaces
One Last Wish (coming soon)

Fluke My Life Series

Running Into Love
Stumbling Into Love

Ruby Falls Series

Falling Fast

Writing as C.A Rose

Alfha Law Series

Justified
Liability
Verdict (coming soon)

Stand-Alone Titles

Finders Keepers

STUMBLING
into LOVE

Aurora Rose Reynolds

Text copyright © 2018 by Aurora Rose Reynolds

Published by Montlake Romance, Seattle

www.apub.com

Amazon, the Amazon logo, and Montlake Romance are trademarks of Amazon.com, Inc., or its affiliates.

ISBN-13: 9781503951983
ISBN-10: 1503951987

Cover design by Letitia Hasser

Printed in the United States of America

Selma & Sejla
May you girls stumble into the most beautiful
kind of love.

Chapter 1

STOOD UP

MAC

Looking around the crowded bar, I pull in a breath. There are lots of people here, and I can tell that most of them have come to have a drink before heading home after a long day at the office—men still wearing their suits, women in skirts and heels with their hair still perfectly styled. This isn't the kind of place where I would normally hang out. There are no TVs playing in the corners of the room with the game on or men drinking beer while talking too loudly. It's too sophisticated for that, with black-and-white photos in elegant frames hanging on the walls depicting Manhattan years ago, when the city was hardly more than a few blocks. Dark wood tables aren't scratched or worn. The leather chairs aren't peeling or falling apart at the seams; they all look new. Everything about this place screams class. Feeling a breeze come from the door, I turn to look at it and let out a disappointed breath when I see a beautiful woman walk in, followed by a good-looking man.

Picking up my cell phone off the top of the bar, I pull up my text messages and check to make sure that I haven't gotten the time or date wrong, that I'm at the right place. Seeing that I am exactly where I'm supposed to be, my hand tightens around the phone in embarrassment.

The guy I was supposed to be meeting for a drink is now thirty minutes late, and he hasn't called or replied to the text I sent more than fifteen minutes ago. So I've officially been stood up. I drop my cell phone into my purse, then drain the glass holding my lemon-drop martini. I feel my face pinch as the sour taste hits my tongue, then I gasp when the vodka burns down my throat.

"Would you like another?" the bartender asks. My watering eyes meet her brown ones.

I should say no and just go home, but I know my sister Libby will be disappointed if I show up not even an hour after my date was supposed to begin. I really don't want to see the pity in her eyes when I tell her Chris didn't show. She was way more excited than I was that I had a date tonight, especially after my self-inflicted dry spell.

"Sure." I give the bartender my answer and a smile. Without a word, she picks up the empty glass and carries it down to the other end of the bar. As I wait for her to come back, the woman reflected in the mirror across from me catches my attention. Even knowing she's me, I still stare in disbelief. When I told Libby I was going out on a date, she insisted on doing my makeup and hair. I didn't fight her like I normally would have because I wanted to make a good impression. I wanted my first date in two years to go well. But I look like a stranger. My hair, normally tied back in a ponytail, is down in a mass of wavy red curls. My eye makeup, normally only mascara, is smoldering and sexy, making me look mysterious. My lips, used to only ChapStick, look full and plump, thanks to the pink stain she used.

I wonder what Edward would think if he saw me right now.

With a deep sigh, I quickly push that thought aside, annoyed with myself for even wondering about him. Edward has been my friend since we met two years ago at a baseball game. We bonded over our love for the Mets and beer. He was easy to talk to, funny and kind. Since that day, I've had a crush on him—and have been trying to no avail to get him to notice me as more than just a friend.

I thought my plan was working until a few weeks ago, when he introduced me to his apparently longtime girlfriend. This caused me to realize the connection I thought we had was all in my head, and that I'd wasted two years of my life waiting for him to see me as more than just a beer-drinking buddy. Which brings me to sitting alone in a bar on a Friday night, all because I wanted to prove that I'm completely over my Edward crush. Well, that and seeing how happy my sister Fawn is with her new boyfriend. I wanted to see if I could find that for myself. So, really, this is all Fawn's fault. If she wasn't so happy, I probably wouldn't have said yes to the first guy who asked me out. Shaking my head, I think about the time Fawn tried to get my other best guy friend, Tex, to ask me out. Not only is he married but happily—and to my good friend Elizabeth. That was embarrassing—but nothing compares with getting stood up tonight.

"Would you like me to start a tab?" The bartender brings me out of my thoughts by dropping a napkin and my drink in front of me on the bar.

"No, thanks." I shake my head and pass her the fifty-dollar bill I got out earlier to cover my first drink.

"Are you sure?"

"Yes, thank you." I smile, and she smiles back while smoothly taking the fifty from me. Picking up my fresh drink, I take a sip and then look toward the door when cool evening air rushes inside. Disappointment hits me when I don't see my date—but that feeling is quickly washed away when my eyes lock on the man coming through the door, and my body tingles from head to toe.

The guy is handsome. No, not handsome. That word doesn't do him justice. He's gorgeous. But not model gorgeous. He's too rough-looking for that. He looks like he's recently spent time in the sun; his dark hair is slightly wavy and curls around his ears and neck, accentuating his strong jaw and full lips. I can't tell the exact color of his eyes from where I'm sitting, but even from a distance they seem bright because of the dark lashes surrounding them. Pulling my eyes down from his face, I take in the expanse of his wide shoulders covered in a plaid shirt and leather jacket and a trim waist encased in a pair of jeans that mold to his thick legs. Drawing my gaze back up to his, I find him studying me with heat in his eyes. I shift in my chair, wondering what it would be like to run my fingers through his hair while he kissed me. Blinking at that forward thought, I shake my head and pull my eyes from his. I look down at my drink before picking it up and downing it in one shot. Hopping off my bar stool, I hold on to the edge of the bar because I'm wobbling in the heels that Libby insisted I borrow. Heels that almost killed me twice on the way to the bar because I can barely walk in them.

Getting the bartender's attention, I point toward the hall that leads to the restrooms at the back of the bar to let her know I'm not taking off. She nods. Making my way through the crowd, I head down a long hallway and get into line behind two blondes who smile at me before resuming their conversation. "So did you finally try the lipstick I sent you?" one of them asks as I pull out my cell phone again to see if I have any missed calls or messages, which I don't.

Stupid men.

"I forgot to tell you!" The other laughs. "I tested it out, and you were right! It didn't come off even after the forty-minute blow job I gave Charles."

Forty-minute blow job? I rub my own jaw just thinking about it.

"I told you it's awesome stuff," the friend replies as the door to the restroom opens and a woman comes out.

"You were right!" the other agrees. Then they both disappear behind the closed door.

Knowing Libby loves makeup, I smile while sending her a text.

I just overheard two women talking about lipstick that doesn't come off when you're giving head. I think you should check it out.

Not even two seconds later, my phone buzzes.

Ummm . . . thank you . . . I think?

It was actually a forty-minute blow job, I clarify.

A forty-minute blow job is way more impressive than lipstick that doesn't come off, she replies.

I giggle, dropping my cell phone back into my bag just as the door opens and the women come out, laughing.

After finishing up in the bathroom, I start back to the front of the bar.

I stop suddenly—when I feel a hand hit my ass hard enough to sting.

"What the hell?" I start to spin around, but my heels wobble once more. Causing me to stumble right into a warm chest that smells like leather and mint.

"Are you all right?" Large hands capture my waist, and I blink up at my savior. Who also happens to be the guy I noticed earlier. One of his arms wraps around me, and he pulls me flush against his solid chest, making every inch of me come to life. "You okay?"

"What?" I ask, in shock.

He drags me up his body, then drops his face closer to mine.

"You okay?" I see his mouth move, but it takes a few seconds to register that he asked if I was okay. All I can seem to focus on is the way it feels to be pressed against him.

"I . . ." I shake my head to clear away the lust that is suddenly overwhelming me. "Yes . . . sorry. Thank you."

"Good." Smiling, he lets me go.

I wonder briefly if it's too late to say I'm *not* okay just so he'll hold on to me for a moment longer.

Sheesh, this guy is deadly.

"Thank you." I bow at the waist while backing away.

He chuckles.

Turning on my heels, I head back for the bar as quickly as I can, thanking my lucky stars that I make it there without incident. I hop up on my stool—luckily still available—then motion for the bartender. As soon as I have her attention, I point at my empty glass. She nods.

"Do you mind if I join you?" I don't even have to look to know who's asking that question. My body reacts to him the same way it did seconds ago. Goose bumps break out across my skin, and a shiver slides down my spine. The guy who has suddenly become the object of all my fantasies slides onto the empty stool next to mine.

"Sure." I shrug, trying to play it cool.

He smiles.

"Wesley." He leans closer to me, and my breathing goes funny.

"Pardon?" His grin shows off a perfect smile and straight, white teeth. I've never thought teeth were attractive until now, but there is something sexy about his.

"Name's Wesley. You are . . . ?" He sticks his large hand out in my direction, and my stomach dances with nervous butterflies as I drop my eyes to it before looking at him once more.

That's when I notice that his eyes are blue, but not just *any* blue. They remind me of the beach out on Long Island near my parents' house, where I spent most of my childhood.

"I'm . . . um . . . Mac . . . Mackenzie," I stutter, placing my hand in his much larger calloused one as I watch him smile.

"Nice to meet you, Mackenzie."

"Uh . . . yeah. Nice to meet you." I nod, feeling his thumb slide over the pulse at my wrist while our eyes stay locked.

"Here's your change, and a fresh drink," the bartender says, breaking the moment.

I pull my eyes and hand from Wesley's as the bartender slides the cash across the top of the bar toward me and sets my new lemon drop down on a fresh napkin.

"Thank you." I clear my throat, trying to get myself under control. This proves to be impossibly hard to do since I can feel Wesley's eyes still on me—as well as his wide-spread knees on either side of my thigh.

"What are you drinking?" the bartender asks him.

I pick up my drink, realizing I need to do something with my hands so I won't fan myself.

"Bud, in the bottle," he says.

I feel his hand come to rest against my lower back and burn into my skin through my sweater.

I try not to look at him.

The bartender bends at the waist and straightens back up a second later with a beer in her hand that she sets in front of him after she opens it.

"Do you want me to start a tab?" she asks.

I watch in the mirror as he lifts his chin and hands her a credit card. She sets it behind the bar at the register before walking off once more to tend to her other customers.

"So what brings you here tonight?" Turning my head toward Wesley at his question, I wonder if I should lie. Then I wonder why the hell I'm wondering that since he doesn't know me anyway. It would make no sense to lie to him.

"I was supposed to meet someone here for a drink, but he stood me up."

"Someone stood *you* up?" he asks, sounding appalled on my behalf.

My lips twitch into a smile as I laugh.

"Yeah."

"Idiot." He shakes his head as his eyes roam over me. He takes a pull from his beer, and my stomach dances once more.

"Why are *you* here?" I ask after a moment, needing to fill the silence that has settled between us.

"I needed a beer." He nods toward the bottle in his hand. "It was a long day."

"Work?" I ask.

He nods once more as his eyes fill with something I can't under-stand yet, but know I don't like. Something about it makes me feel uneasy, like I want to protect him.

"Sorry," I say softly, fighting the urge to reach out and touch him.

"Don't be. I've got a cold beer in my hand, and I'm talking to a beautiful woman. Gotta say, my day's looking up."

The word *beautiful* makes me feel a little bit guilty. He has no idea that the woman he's sitting with isn't who I really am. I don't normally look like this or drink martinis. He doesn't know that I prefer to drink beer and never wear makeup unless I have to. Even the clothes I have on aren't mine. They're Libby's. My closet consists of mostly T-shirts and jeans. I want to tell him all that, but I don't. Instead, I decide to pretend for a little while longer that I'm someone else, that I'm the kind of woman a man who looks like he does would be interested in.

Two hours later, as I settle into the backseat of a cab with Wesley next to me, I wonder what the hell I'm doing.

I've had only two lovers in my life—both of them long-term boy-friends I didn't sleep with until months into the relationship. I don't do one-night stands. Or at least I've never had one before, but something came over me when Wesley asked if I wanted to get out of the bar. I don't even think I realized that something inside me knew if I didn't go with him, I would regret it for the rest of my life.

The door slams, and I listen as Wesley gives the driver directions to his place. I'm suddenly unsure of my decision.

"Hey." His voice washes over me while his hand moves up my leg to the junction between my thighs.

My pulse quickens, and white-hot lust shoots through my system. The same lust I've been feeling all night. Meeting his gaze, I see that the same lust is staring right back at me. Licking my suddenly dry lips, I watch as his eyes drop to my mouth. A whoosh of breath leaves my lungs as he leans in.

The first touch of his lips to mine is soft and exploratory—a tease of what's to come. Touching my tongue to his bottom lip, I feel his chest vibrate against mine. I whimper as he deepens the kiss, thrusting his tongue into my mouth to toy with mine while his hand in the hair at the back of my head tightens and tilts it, sending a sting of desire through me.

Pulling back when the cab comes to a stop, I pant as he pays the driver. I take his hand when he offers it and allow him to help me out of the backseat. Shutting the door behind us, he keeps my hand firmly in his as we walk down the sidewalk and toward a set of stairs that leads to the bottom level of a townhouse. After he unlocks and opens the door, I start to walk inside ahead of him. He stops me, wraps his hand around my waist, and moves his face close to mine. He's so close that I can feel his warm breath brush against my lips as he speaks.

"You sure about this?" he asks.

My pulse, already thundering away, speeds up.

"Yes," I whisper without having to think about my answer. Raising my shaking hands, I run my fingers through his hair. It's just as soft and as thick as I thought it would be. I pull his mouth down toward mine.

Groaning, "Fuck," his mouth captures mine as his hands slide down my back to my ass. He cups it, then lifts me off the ground like I weigh nothing at all. Wrapping my legs around his hips, I moan into his mouth. He walks us into his apartment, kicking the door shut behind us.

～

When I blink my eyes open, the early-morning light greets me through the partially opened blinds next to the bed. I realize I'm not home; then I feel the heavy weight of Wesley's arm draped over my bare waist. I pull in a quiet breath and let it out slowly as I look around. The room is small—just big enough for the queen-size bed I'm lying on and a dresser tucked in the corner. There are no curtains covering the windows or pictures on the walls. There's nothing to tell me anything about the man I just spent the night with. The man who held me throughout the night, the man still curled around me.

Worrying my bottom lip, I debate what I should do now that I'm awake. The idea of having to face Wesley when he wakes up sends panic pulsing through my system. I know enough from talking to friends that the morning after is always awkward for both parties, and I want to save us both that experience. Figuring it's better to get out now, I carefully move out of his grasp. This isn't easy to do because his hold on me seems to tighten whenever I make any leeway. Finally extracting myself from him and the bed, I quietly get up and search through our clothes—scattered across the floor—until I find my stuff.

Once I have everything in my arms, I head for the bedroom door. I pause with my hand on the doorknob and look back at the bed. Running my eyes over Wesley's dark hair, his face relaxed in sleep, and his big, strong body makes something uncomfortable shift in my stomach. It's like my soul is telling me that I'm an idiot for just taking off and not seeing what will happen if I stick around.

Shaking off that feeling, I quietly open the door and step out, closing it behind me. Walking into his living-room-slash-kitchen, I put on my clothes as fast as I can. I grab my bag and toss it over my shoulder. Nibbling my bottom lip some more, I wonder if I should leave him a note. I close my eyes at the ridiculousness of the thought. What would it even say? "Thanks for last night?" "It was fun?" Yes, we had a good time, but he had a good time with the Mackenzie who dresses sexy, wears makeup, and drinks martinis. He wasn't with the real me. Mac the tomboy. The beer drinker, the girl who is always just one of the guys.

My eyes sting at that realization. I like Wesley, but he has no idea who I really am. I doubt that he would like me if he did.

As I leave his apartment, I stop at the top of the steps on the sidewalk and look both ways. I'm not far from the train, so instead of getting a cab like I planned on doing, I make my way toward the subway station at the end of the block. I swipe my MetroCard, then take the stairs down into the mostly empty platform.

Since it's Saturday, I know it might be a while before my train arrives. I take a seat on one of the benches lining the wall, then dig through my bag for my phone and come up empty-handed. I close my eyes and grit my teeth.

I know I had my phone when I was with Wesley because I sent a text to Libby to let her know not to worry about me. I typed that message in Wesley's bed while he tried to distract me with his mouth and hands, something he succeeded in doing two seconds after I pressed "Send."

Groaning, I drop my face to my hands. I left it back at his place.

"Now what?" I ask myself aloud.

I can't go back and knock on his door. I would look like a complete idiot if I did that.

What would I say? "Hey! I just snuck out of your bed and apartment, but I came back because I think I left my phone behind. Can I come in and search for it?"

"Google is the answer." Pulling my hands away from my face, I sit back and look at the man standing in front of me. His white hair is wild and sticking out in every direction, his face is pale, and his clothes are dirty and torn. "Google is always the answer. Follow Google."

He twists his neck back and forth as he gets closer to where I'm sitting. Seeing the way his eyes are dilated and the pulse in his neck is thumping away, I know he's high. Meaning he's unstable. My dad has always told me never to show fear, never to allow anyone to think they can intimidate me. That has always stuck with me. I raise my chin, and he stops moving, but I don't relax. I know better than to let my guard down. Sliding my hand into the pocket of my coat, I wrap my fingers tightly around my can of mace and stand up.

He doesn't move, but his eyes stay locked on me as I slowly back away from him down the platform toward a young couple who is making out and an older gentleman who is reading the paper. Hearing the sound of the train rushing through the tunnel, I sigh in relief when I see that it's mine. As soon as the train stops and the doors open, I get into a crowded car and take a seat across from the doors. I watch them shut as the train pulls away.

A flash of black catches my attention, and I turn my head. My eyes widen when I see Wesley. He's wearing a pair of gray sweats, a black hoodie, and sneakers—and he's running down the platform after my train. I stand without thinking, and his disappointed eyes meet mine through the window right before he disappears out of sight as we head into the tunnel.

Taking my seat again, I close my eyes, lean my head back, and tuck my purse in front of my stomach. I hold it there tightly, trying to stop a wave of nausea.

He came after me.

I don't know how he knew I would be getting on the train, but he did.

He came after me. Or at least I think he did.

I furrow my brow, then feel my heart plummet when I realize he probably found my phone and was just trying to catch me so he could return it. Opening my eyes again, I take a deep breath. I need to figure out how to get my phone from him. It will be more awkward than waking up with him, but I can't afford to buy a new one.

As soon as I reach my stop, I head up the steps out of the station and then walk the three blocks to my place. Libby and I share a one-bedroom apartment on the second floor of a three-family house. The house is a traditional New York City brownstone, with a wide stoop in the front. In the summer, I sit there and watch the kids in the neighborhood play as I drink my coffee in the mornings.

I got the apartment when I moved to New York. It was the only thing I ever had that was just mine, the first thing I didn't have to share with my sisters. Well, until Fawn came to the city to go to college. Libby joined us not long after that. Thankfully, Fawn no longer lives with us. I love my sisters, but the three of us sharing the small space led to a lot of fights.

As soon as I'm inside the foyer, I stop at the mailboxes and open mine. Pulling out a handful of mostly junk mail, I see Miss Ina open her apartment door an inch to peek out to see who's in the hall. Doing the nice thing, I give her a smile. I regret it instantly, because she takes it as an invitation to open the door completely. Miss Ina is eighty years old, a tiny thing with a humpback that makes her appear even smaller than she already is. Her white hair looks like a big puffy cloud on top of her head, and her frail skin is practically transparent, but her brown eyes are so dark, they look almost black. I swear when she looks at you, it's like she's looking into your soul. Scanning it for all the wrongs you've done in your life. Nothing happens in the house without her knowing about it. She knows everyone's business—sometimes before they even do.

"We need to talk," she says as she pushes her walker in front of her and moves out into the entryway.

"How can I help you, Miss Ina?" I ask, watching her hobble closer with her walker squeaking as she sidles up to me.

"I can't sleep with all the banging around upstairs."

"Miss Ina, we've talked about this. The house is old. It's not sound-proof. Libby and I both try to be quiet, but you can't expect us to tiptoe around upstairs all the time," I say as nicely as I can.

She huffs. I do feel bad for her. I know exactly what she's going through, since there's a family who lives above *us* with three small children. We can hear everything they do upstairs—and I mean *everything*—from the kids playing with cars on the floor to Mrs. and Mr. Kind's bed banging against the wall at night as they work on a fourth baby.

"I need my rest. You girls need to be more considerate of your neighbors," she says.

I sigh. I've been down this road with her enough times to know that she won't give up until I agree, even if I don't really agree with her.

I give in. "We will try to be quieter."

She huffs again in response. Giving up on making her happy because it's impossible, I tuck my mail into my bag and scoot around her and her walker. I move toward the stairs.

"Have a great day, Miss Ina!" I call over my shoulder when I'm half-way up the first flight. She doesn't respond—not that I expected her to.

Unlocking the door to my apartment, I push it open and listen to it groan. I step inside and shut it behind me. Okay, I slam it a little to get it to close—and to piss off Ina. I shrug off my purse and jacket, then lay both of them on the couch. Next, I take off my boots and drop them to the floor near the couch. The apartment is small, just about four hundred square feet. The living room is just inside the front door and is barely big enough for the couch that sits under the pass-through window into the kitchen. The TV is directly across from it. The kitchen is also tiny, but it works for Libby and me since neither of us can cook. The apartment might not be fabulous, but the bathroom is amazing—or rather, my bathtub is. The old claw-foot tub is the only reason I haven't moved out.

Knowing Libby is at work, I start to undress as I make my way into the bathroom. I have always loved taking baths, and a bath is exactly what I need to relax after the morning's excitement. Filling up the tub, I dump a handful of bath salts into the water, then climb in. After an hour of soaking, I get out and put on a pair of sweats and a T-shirt. I plant myself on the couch in front of the TV with a bowl of Cheerios. I tell myself that I won't worry about getting my phone back from Wesley until after the weekend.

But I do worry, and when I'm not worrying, I spend every moment thinking about him.

Chapter 2

THAT SO WASN'T PART OF THE PLAN

MAC

Over the past few days, I've thought of a hundred different ways I might be able to get my phone back from Wesley without actually having to see him face-to-face. First I thought about breaking into his place and stealing it, but I don't think that would go over well—he would know it was me if all that was missing was my phone. I also thought about asking my sisters to help me out by dressing up like cable repair workers, but they would ask too many questions, so I don't bother. I was at a loss until this morning when an idea came to me—a lame idea, but an idea all the same.

After I got ready, I left my place and made a couple of stops before getting on the train to Wesley's. When I reach the steps in front of his apartment, I look around to make sure the coast is clear before taking the stairs down to his door. I drop my purse on the bottom step, and I get out the note I wrote, the prepaid envelope I just bought, and some clear packing tape. I unroll a section of tape, press the envelope and note to the door, then tape across the top of them. Realizing I have to use my teeth to rip the tape because I don't have scissors, I get up on my tiptoes to bite it. It's too high for me to reach with my mouth. As I start to pull the envelope from the door, the roll of tape falls from my grasp and hits the ground, then rolls away from me.

"Dammit!" I hiss as it wraps around itself and my hand. Ripping the envelope off the door, I try to untangle myself from the mess of clear packing tape, cringing at the obnoxious noise it makes.

"Do you need some help?"

"Shit!" I shout as I spin around.

When I look up, my eyes meet Wesley's. He's more gorgeous than I remember. He also looks slightly annoyed, with his arms crossed over his massive chest and his blue eyes locked on me.

"You're here . . . ," I say like an idiot, feeling my face get hot.

"I live here." He lifts his chin toward the door. "What are *you* doing here?"

"I . . . I was just in the neighborhood," I lie while wrapping the tape into a ball around the roll in my hands.

Moving his eyes from my face to the roll of tape in my hands, he asks, "What were you doing?"

"I was . . ." My words taper off as he drops his eyes to the ground. He bends down to pick up the note I was going to leave him.

Wesley, sorry I missed you. I think I left my phone behind when we hung out. Can you put it in the envelope and drop it in the nearest mailbox?

Thank you, Mackenzie

He reads it aloud. My cheeks, which were already hot, burn hotter as he lifts his head to look at me.

"Did you ring the bell?" he asks.

I look at the door behind me, then back at him.

"Bell?"

"The doorbell—did you ring it?"

"Um . . ."

"It's hooked up to my cell phone, so when someone rings the bell, my phone rings."

"Maybe it's broken?" I suggest lamely, tipping my head to the side and hoping I look innocent.

He takes two steps down, presses the button, and his phone chimes immediately.

Darn it.

"Doesn't seem broken to me." He turns around to face me, his huge body making the small alcove we're in seem even smaller.

Knowing I don't have a good excuse, I keep my mouth closed. My eyes widen involuntarily as he closes the minute distance between us with his eyes locked on mine.

"Wesley . . . ," I breathe when his familiar scent fills my lugs. His warmth seems to wrap around me even though he doesn't touch me.

"You slipped out on me. Why?" The question is soft, but there is no mistaking the annoyance and frustration in his voice or his eyes as he waits for my answer.

I won't be giving him an honest answer, because saying why I left the way I did out loud would be ridiculous now that I'm standing in front of him.

"I . . . fuck"—he rips his hand through his hair—"I can't believe you just took off without a word."

My eyes close briefly. I open my mouth to say something, anything.

Before I can, he cuts me off with a shake of his head and a sharp "Never mind."

Turning his back to me, he opens the door and goes inside. I swallow the mass of emotions I'm feeling as I stand in the open doorway, wondering what I should do next. Pulling in a much-needed breath, I shove the ball of tape into my bag and pick it up before moving into his apartment. I didn't really stop to look around the last time I was here. Seeing it now, I realize I didn't miss out on much. The kitchen is small, with only a round table and two chairs in the middle of it. In the living room, there is a row of boxes stacked up against the wall, a big comfortable-looking gray couch, and a large TV on a plain black stand. The whole space is empty of anything personal—there are no pictures or anything else to make it homey. I wonder if they are in the boxes still to be unpacked.

"Here," he rumbles, holding out my phone.

Turning to face him, I reach out slowly and take my phone. I shove it in the pocket of my jacket while I avoid his eyes.

"Thank you."

"Sure."

"I'm sorry," I say quietly. "I . . ."

"I don't want to hear it," he replies, cutting me off before I can say more.

I fight the urge to flinch.

"I don't want to hear whatever bullshit excuse you're going to try to feed me."

"Excuse me?" I lift my head to look at him.

"You heard me." He holds my stare.

I feel my eyes narrow, and his do the same in return.

"You got your phone. That's why you came, right? So why are you still standing here?"

"Wow." I shake my head, pull my eyes away from his. "You're a dick."

"You couldn't get enough of my dick the other night, baby. If I remember correctly, you begged me for it more than once," he says.

My head snaps back toward him. "Jerk!" I hiss, lifting a hand to smack him.

He catches it before I make contact. I lift my other hand to try again, but he catches that one, too, and then pulls them both up above my head. Breathing heavily, I stare at him. He stares back.

"Now what?" he says with a smirk.

18

I do the only thing I can think of. I raise myself up on my tiptoes and press my mouth to his. I expect my move to knock him off balance—and down a peg or two—but that doesn't happen. Instead, his mouth captures mine, and his tongue slips between my parted lips. I don't fight the kiss. Just like last time, I discover I want this more than I want anything. I want *him*.

Releasing one of my hands, he wraps his arm around my waist and pulls me flush against him. His mouth travels down my jaw to my neck. He bites it softly, making my toes curl. Feeling the pull of arousal deep in my belly, I tug at his shirt until it's free from his jeans, then run my hand up his abs before dragging my nails down over the ridges and valleys there.

"Wesley . . . ," I whimper as his tongue flicks across my neck.

The next thing I know, his breath whispers across the shell of my ear.

"Tell me you want this." He presses his erection into my stomach, letting me know he's ready to repeat what happened the other night. "Tell me you want me."

"I want you," I moan just as his mouth captures mine once more.

His hands rip at my clothes, and mine do the same to his in return. Hearing my jacket and top hit the floor, I urge his shirt up and over his head, then move my hands to the button of his jeans. He walks us backward, toward his room. He gets his pants down over his hips before he pulls away from me.

"Kick off your shoes." With a jerky nod, I work my feet out of my sneakers. I bite my lip as he pulls down my pants and panties in one move, then slides his hands up my thighs, along my sides, and then around my back to remove my bra. He lets it fall to the floor without a second glance.

Standing completely naked in front of him, I fight the urge to hide myself from his heated gaze as it roams over every inch of me. It makes me feel hot and restless.

"Why'd you sneak out on me?" he asks, cupping my sex. I swallow hard as heat pools between my legs.

"I . . ." My head falls back, and a moan slips past my lips as his fingers slide through my slick folds.

"Look at me."

I lift my head and meet his gaze. My heart speeds up when I register the dark need in his eyes.

"Why?" His thumb circles my sensitive clit, and my hips jerk into his touch.

"I don't know," I whimper, trying to force his fingers to give me more.

"Why?" he repeats as my back hits the bed.

He lands on top of me and uses his knees to spread my legs farther apart.

"I don't know."

"Stop lying to me," he growls while thrusting two fingers deep inside me.

I cry out in bliss as they curve up, hitting me exactly where I need them to.

"Why'd you leave?"

"Wesley . . ."

"Why?"

"Because you wouldn't want me if you really knew me," I admit on a gasp.

His fingers speed up in response.

"Oh god."

My back arches high off the bed. He pulls my breast into his mouth, scraping his teeth across my nipple before releasing it.

"I do want you."

"You wouldn't if you really knew me," I pant as my nails scrape down his cut abs and wrap around his hard length. I stroke once, then twice more, before he pulls himself from my grasp.

"You're wrong." His mouth hovers over mine. "So fucking wrong." His words whisper across my lips as he thrusts inside me hard, sending me sliding up the bed. Digging my heels into the backs of his thighs, I wrap one arm around his broad shoulders and thread the fingers of my other hand through his hair. Taking my mouth again in a deep kiss, he pulls out slowly—so slowly that I feel every inch of him as my walls ripple around his length.

"Please," I beg, tearing my mouth from his.

"What do you need?" he asks, sliding his hand between us and finding my clit once more with his thumb.

"Harder!" I plead.

His eyes flash, but he doesn't stop the slow, steady torture.

"Please." I lift my hips, trying to force him to give me what I want.

"You want more of my cock?"

"Yes! Please fuck me!" I don't know where those words come from, but as soon as they are out, his pace picks up and his mouth takes mine again. Kissing him back, I moan against his tongue.

He sends me over the edge, and I shatter into a million pieces.

Slowly coming back to myself, I blink open my eyes to find him completely still and looking down at me.

"This time, keep your eyes open and on mine when you come," he says, lifting my back off the bed and settling back on his calves while positioning me so I'm sitting on his lap. He pushes one hand into my hair to keep my head in place and locks the other around my back, holding me flush against him.

"Oh . . . ," I breathe as he moves his hips up into mine, sending a whole new wave of sensations through me.

Grabbing hold of his shoulders for leverage, I do my best to move my hips in sync with his. It's hard to concentrate on what I'm doing, though, as he looks into my eyes like he's searching for something. Needing to break eye contact, I try to kiss him. His hold only tightens, keeping my head in place as his hips jerk faster and his arm around my waist brings me down hard, forcing my orgasm closer.

"Wesley."

"Give it to me."

It's as if his voice actually commands my body. I give in and let go. With my eyes locked on his, I watch his heated gaze as his hips jerk.

"Mine," he groans as he comes.

Releasing my hair, he tucks my face against his neck by pushing his palm against the back of my head. Holding me close. Making me feel safe and protected.

The sound of both of us breathing heavily fills my ears as his heartbeat pounds against the damp skin of my chest. Swallowing, I close my eyes, which are filling with tears.

I have no idea what the hell just happened. Well, that's not true—I *do* know what happened, but sleeping with him *again* was so totally not part of the plan I came up with this morning.

"Fuck," he whispers in a grated tone.

That brings me back to the situation at hand. I pull back and look at him.

"Um . . . ?"

"I didn't use a condom."

I blink at his statement as what he says sinks in. My pulse skyrockets.

"I'm clean. I get tested every six months—and I haven't been with anyone in longer than that."

"I . . ." I close my eyes, then open them back up. "Me neither. I . . . I'm clean, too . . ." I look away from him as his words replay in my head over and over, at loudspeaker volume, reminding me of how stupid I am.

"I'm sorry, gorgeous . . ." He gives me a tight squeeze. "I didn't even think. I—"

"I'm not on birth control," I blurt out, cutting off whatever he was going to say.

I see him flinch when he realizes what that could mean.
This cannot be happening.

I lift my hips away from his, mourning the loss of him as I do. I scramble out of his grasp and stumble off the bed, almost falling on my face.

"Where the fuck are you going?"

His sharp tone stops me in my tracks. I look up to find him sitting on the side of the bed—in all his perfect, naked glory.

"I have to go to work." I pull nervously at my hair with shaking hands, then gesture between us. "This"—I swallow—"wasn't a part of my plan . . ."

"Part of your *plan?*" His eyes narrow and hold mine.

I bite my lip, then shake my head. I wonder why the hell my brain and mouth are not cooperating with me.

I tie my hair back up into a ponytail and finally release my lip.

"I didn't think you'd be home. I . . . I have to get to work," I explain as I put on my bra, then pick up my panties and pants. As I put them on, I avoid looking at him again even though I can sense him watching my every move. I bend down to slip on my socks and sneakers, and out of the corner of my eye, I see him leave the room.

He comes back a second later, pushing a piece of paper under my nose.

"What's this?"

"My number. Your cell's dead, and you're taking off again. I'm giving it to you so you'll have it if something comes up."

If something comes up? Like if I'm pregnant?

He's not giving it to me so that I will call him. That hurt. Actually, that killed.

My stomach turns as I whisper, "Right." I shove the piece of paper into my pocket.

Skirting him, I step into the living room, pick up my top and jacket, and put both on quickly before grabbing my bag.

I feel his fingers wrap around my wrist. I stop midstep. I swear I see hurt in his eyes when I look up at him, but I brush that thought aside, knowing I must be seeing things.

".Call me," he says softly.

I swallow. "Sure."

I shake off his hold, then head for the door. I try to make it look like I'm not running away when that is exactly what I'm doing. As soon as I'm outside and on the sidewalk, I hail the first cab I see, get in the backseat, and let out the breath I've been holding. I give the driver directions. Thankfully, the morning rush hour is over so it doesn't take me long to get uptown.

I arrive at work a little less than thirty minutes late, unlock my office door, and head inside, flipping on the lights as I go. My dad and I painted the front of my office a calming, soft blue that goes well with the abstract art prints I framed and hung on the walls. Across from my desk, against the opposite wall, are two golden-brown chairs with cool-looking wooden arms. They match the coffee table in front of them, where several magazines are splayed out. Blowing out a breath, I head toward my desk.

Days like today, I'm thankful I'm my own boss so I don't have anyone to answer to. Taking the leap by starting my own massage-therapy business was one of the scariest things I've ever done, but so far there hasn't been a day I've regretted it.

I love what I do. I love making people feel good and helping them relax. When I was younger, I used to get migraines so bad I would become physically ill. The doctors couldn't do anything for me, so my mom did some research and found out that a lot of people were able to find relief with massage. I was skeptical, but after my first session, I left feeling normal and clear-minded—unlike when I took medication. That day, I became a believer. I knew that I wanted to help people the way I had been helped.

Once I get some incense burning, I take off my coat. I drape it over the back of my chair, then take a seat at my desk. I rest my forehead on the cool wood as tears fill my eyes again. I shouldn't care as much as I do that things with Wesley ended the way they did, but that does nothing to stop the stabbing pain I feel in my chest.

It takes longer than I'm comfortable with to get myself under control, but after a few deep breaths, I sit up and pull his number out of my pocket. I try to memorize it before opening the top drawer in my desk and dropping it in, hoping I will never have to use it. I dig my cell phone out of my pocket and plug it in to charge, then head for the bathroom to clean up.

I have a few clients coming in today, so I figure that will help keep my mind busy until I leave the office. Then I'll head out to visit my parents and sisters on Long Island for the Thanksgiving holiday. I'm now looking forward to going—they will be the distraction I so desperately need.

~

Standing in my parents' kitchen the next morning, I lean against the counter with a cup of coffee in my hand, listening to my mom blabber on about the new neighbor who moved in a couple of houses down. Mom's working on the pies for Thanksgiving tomorrow.

"He's single. Maybe you could go over and introduce yourself to him," she suggests, looking at me expectantly.

I hear Libby giggle from her perch on one of the stools at the island in front of us. She *would* think it's funny that our mom is trying to hook me up with a fifty-year-old man she knows nothing about. It's not happening to *her*.

"I'm not interested in dating anyone right now, Mom," I mutter.

I take a sip of coffee.

"Are you a lesbian?"

I almost spit it out but instead suck it down the wrong pipe and choke on it. "What?" I cough, wipe away the coffee dribbling from my bottom lip, and grab a paper towel so I can wipe the rest off my hand and shirt.

"You haven't been on a date in forever. I never hear you talk about any men that you are interested in. I'm just wondering if maybe you're—"

"I'm not." I cut off her next words. "God, Mom. Seriously?" I throw my free hand up in the air before dropping it back down to my side. "I don't want to date, so I'm automatically a lesbian?"

"Well, there is nothing wrong with it if you are. You can't blame me for asking." She scrunches up her nose as Libby laughs harder.

"What's going on?" Fawn asks, coming into the kitchen a second later.

She's wearing her normal attire—a sweater and leggings with a pair of Toms on her feet. Her blonde, curly hair, currently tied up on top of her head, makes her seem pixielike. I swear she's glowing. She looks happy, really happy. I know it has to do with the man she's been dating for a few weeks. Levi, her neighbor—a hot cop who moved in next door to her weeks ago. A hot cop who looks at my sister like she was put on the earth just for him.

God, why does that make me jealous?

"What is it?" Fawn repeats, looking at Libby, who's still laughing like a crazy woman.

"I suggested that your sister go over and introduce herself to Brent. He just moved into the Manors' old place."

"Oh . . . ?" Fawn says, looking at me.

She's clearly confused, not understanding why that would make Libby laugh like a hyena.

"Mac said she's not interested, so Mom asked her if she was a lesbian!" Libby fills in the blanks through her laughter.

I shoot daggers at her.

"Ohhh." Fawn's lips twitch into a smile before she starts laughing, too. She covers her mouth as she does.

"You *would* think it's funny—because it's not you!" I mutter, annoyed with all of them.

My mom's statement doesn't surprise me. She's crazy. And dead set on getting us girls married off so she can get to the grandkids.

Good luck with that.

"I know Fawn's not a lesbian. She's sleeping with Levi," Mom states matter-of-factly. Fawn's eyes get big. "How is he in bed, honey?"

"Mom!" Fawn hisses as her face turns bright red.

"Yeah, how is he in bed?" Libby asks, sitting forward expectantly.

"I'm not talking to you guys about my sex life . . . ever," Fawn states.

I laugh, earning a glare from her before she walks over to the fridge, opens it up, and grabs a soda.

"My girls are all so hush-hush! Sheesh, can't a mom know that her girls are happy anymore?" Mom gripes.

I roll my eyes at Fawn. She does the same in return.

"When I *have* a sex life, I will talk to you about it, Mom," Libby says.

Mom smiles at her. How my baby sister remains so innocent always surprises me. She is the kind of girl most of the men I know fantasize about—tall, thin, with dark hair and crystal-blue eyes that always look mysterious.

"That's why you're my favorite." Mom reaches across the counter and pats her cheek.

"I know," Libby agrees.

I fight the urge to laugh. My mom does this to us all the time, claiming that one is her favorite if it suits her—when I know for a fact that she loves us all equally.

"Is Levi home?" I ask Fawn when she takes a seat on the stool next to Libby.

As soon as I ask about him, I see her face soften.

God, she's in love.

I don't even think she knows it, but she is totally crazy about him. It's written all over her pretty face.

"Yeah. He's going to be home alone for the holiday since he's on call."

"That sucks," Libby states.

I nod in agreement. It does suck that he'll have to be alone tomorrow, especially when his family lives in Connecticut and Fawn will be here with us. I can't imagine having to be alone during the holidays.

"You should go back and spend Thanksgiving with him," Mom says, surprising all of us with the suggestion.

"I . . ." Fawn opens her mouth, then closes it.

"I don't like the idea of him spending the day alone," Mom continues before Fawn can say more. "I'm sure he'd enjoy having your company."

"You and Dad wouldn't be upset about me leaving to go spend Thanksgiving with my new boyfriend?"

"No," Mom says.

Fawn smiles for a second, then frowns at her.

"Are you sure?"

"Honey, I wouldn't suggest it if I wasn't."

"I'll think about it," Fawn says.

I can see in her eyes that she's already made up her mind. She'll be back in Manhattan before the night is over. Not that I can blame her. If I had a man, I would want to be with him, too. At that thought, Wesley flashes through my mind. I hold my cup of coffee tighter.

I doubt I will ever see him again. That's for the best. Right?

As we load into my parents' car the next morning, I think for the hundredth time that this is a really bad idea. Fawn did go back to Manhattan to be with Levi, which I knew she would do. What I didn't expect was having my mom come into my old room to wake me up and tell me that I needed to get up and get ready. Her plan is to make us all head into the city to surprise Fawn and Levi with Thanksgiving dinner. I tried to tell both my parents we shouldn't, but neither of them will listen to me.

"How mad do you think Fawn will be?" Libby asks as she gets into the backseat with me and buckles in.

"I'm not sure."

I look over my shoulder, out the back window at the two cars parked behind us. My aunts, uncles, and cousins are all piling into their own cars so they can follow us. "I doubt she's going to be *mad*, but I bet she and Levi will be shocked to see so many people at their front door before it's even nine in the morning."

"I tried to text Fawn, but she hasn't messaged back. She must still be sleeping."

"Well, she won't be sleeping for much longer," I state drily.

"True." Libby laughs.

"Are we all ready?" Dad asks as he folds himself in behind the steering wheel.

"Yep, all ready!" Mom sings as she gets into the passenger seat.

Dad starts up the car.

"Are you guys *sure* about this?" I ask.

Mom frowns at me over her shoulder. "Of course! Family should spend the holidays together."

I know the look in her eye—it means there will be no changing her mind. I shake my head and dig my cell phone out of my bag. I send a message to Fawn, letting her know that we are all on our way—and to prepare Levi for a Reed-family Thanksgiving.

∾

"Breathe." I rub my hand down Fawn's back as she attempts to suck in air with her head tucked between her knees. "It will be okay," I insist. I have no idea if I'm right or not.

After we arrived—and after Levi finally answered the door, surprised to see his new girlfriend's family—we settled in, put away groceries, and stared to cook. When I was making coffee, Levi told me to go check on Fawn.

His family had also decided to show up and surprise him for Thanksgiving, and she was freaking out. So here I am, trying to comfort my sister as she sits on the side of the bed, having a panic attack.

"His mom is here. Our mom is here. This means I might as well consider my relationship with him over and done. I have no doubt Mom is going to say something to Levi's parents that will make them forbid him to continue dating me."

"It won't be that bad."

"Do you not remember just weeks ago when Levi met our parents? Mom told me I should get knocked up by him!" She pauses and pulls in a deep breath before lifting her head to look at me. *"In front of him!"* she screeches.

"Levi thought that was funny," I remind her as she assumes her previous position.

"Yeah, but that doesn't mean his family would have! What if something like that happens again? Dinner is going to be a disaster. What if someone starts talking about gravy, and then Mom uses that as a double entendre for Levi's baby batter?"

"Baby batter?" I frown, not sure what she means.

She lifts her head and blinks at me. "His sperm."

"Oh . . . ohhhhh." My face scrunches up.

She lets out a huff of air.

"Listen, whatever happens, you and Levi will be fine. His parents will love you, so you have nothing to worry about."

"Are you sure?"

"Positive. Now finish getting ready, and come on." I stand and pull her up by her hands. "Let's go."

"Right." She shakes out her arms, then twists her neck side to side like she's getting ready for a WWF match. "Let's go."

I follow her out of Levi's bedroom and out of his apartment. In the hall, I stand back and out of the way while she meets Levi's family. Seeing that she's okay, I head into her apartment, where I find Libby hanging out watching TV with Fawn's dog, Muffin. My aunts are busy working in the kitchen.

"Hey, girl." I give Muffin a quick rubdown when she comes over to me, then lead her back across the room.

"Did Fawn finally come out of the bedroom?" Libby asks as I take a seat next to her on the couch.

"She did, but you will never believe what happened."

"What?" She presses "Pause" on the remote, then turns to face me.

"Levi's family showed up."

"Shut up."

"Cross my heart. They just got here."

"Is she okay?" she asks, looking toward the door.

"Yeah. She was panicking, but she's okay now."

"Well, dinner is going to be interesting for sure," she mumbles under her breath. I nod in agreement.

I have no idea just how true that statement is going to be.

~

"Mac!" Levi calls from across the room as soon as I walk into his apartment.

"Give me one second!" I shout back. I'm carrying a pie dish in my arms, so I take it into the kitchen and set it down on the counter.

"What's up?" When I turn around, my entire world comes to a stop. I'm face-to-face with Wesley.

"Wh—" I start to ask what he's doing there, but Levi cuts me off.

"Mac, I want you to meet my partner, Wesley. Wesley, this is Fawn's sister, Mac. Or Mackenzie."

"Partner?" I whisper, staring at him while he stares back. I have no idea what to do. It's so awkward after the way we left each other.

"Are you okay?" Fawn asks, touching my arm.

This snaps me out of it. I pull my gaze from Wesley's to look at her.

"Yeah." I blink and shake my head. "Sorry."

I look at Wesley—or more accurately, I look at his ear—and mutter, "Sorry. It's nice to meet you."

I don't offer to shake his hand. I don't know what would happen if we were to touch again.

"You too," he says.

I can hear the anger in his tone, and I fight back a cringe. I turn to face Fawn again.

"Mom said it's time to get stuff set up so everyone can eat soon," I remind her.

"Crap! The turkey!" she blurts out, turning to Levi. She rises up on tiptoe so she can kiss his cheek. "Get Wesley a beer," she tells him. She looks at Wesley. "I'm glad you could come."

"Thanks," Wesley replies.

She smiles at him, then grabs my hand. "I need your help."

"Sure."

I follow her out of Levi's place, breathing a sigh of relief that I wasn't forced to be around Wesley for much longer. He fills me with too many mixed emotions.

I don't know if I want to curl myself up against his chest or kick him in the shin. Who am I kidding? I definitely want to do both.

Chapter 3

MINE!

WESLEY

Grinding my teeth, I fight the urge to walk across the room and kiss the woman who has been haunting me for the last week. I can't get her out of my head no matter how many times I kick my own ass all over the place. I still want her when I know I shouldn't. She's made it perfectly clear by taking off on me twice without looking back that she doesn't want anything more from me. Unfortunately, my dick hasn't gotten that memo.

Pulling my eyes from her, I try to focus on what Aiden is saying. Aiden, who also happens to be her dad. Fuck . . . How the hell did I end up in this situation?

I try to think by running my hand through my hair. I obviously had no idea when my partner, Levi, invited me over for Thanksgiving that I would be spending the day with Mackenzie's family. If I had known that, I wouldn't have shown.

Who the hell am I kidding? Of course I would have come—because I'm a fucking idiot who enjoys self-inflicted torture. There is something about Mackenzie, or Mac, as her family calls her, that I can't get out of my head. It's not that she's beautiful, even though she is. No, it's something else. She's a mystery I want to solve. I want to find out what kind of woman she really is. Is she the sex kitten I met the first night, or the sporty girl standing a few feet away from me now, wearing worn jeans that fit her like a second skin and a long-sleeve top with the Mets logo on the front of it?

Taking a swig from my beer, I lock eyes with her. Her cheeks get pink across the room before she looks away. When her sister Fawn introduced us earlier, I could tell she was shocked to see me—and worried I'd disclose that we had met before, which annoys me since that's exactly what I wanted to do.

I wanted to kiss her, to touch her in some way. But I had to hold myself back from doing just that. I have never felt a connection to another woman like the one I feel with her. Yes, the sex was unbelievable. The best I've ever had, but that's not why I want her.

There's something vulnerable about her, and that vulnerability calls to the protector in me. From the first moment I saw her in the bar, looking alone and lost, I gravitated to her. Then, after spending two hours talking and laughing with her, I knew I wanted more. More of her laughter, more of her wit, and more of her time. A hell of a lot more time. Which is why I chased after her when I woke up alone after the night we shared.

Feeling her eyes on me once more, I look at her again. I see a hint of arousal that she tries to hide, but it's too late. I see it there, calling to me like a beacon. I don't understand her at all. One minute she's looking at me like she wants to rip off my clothes. The next she's trying to get away from me as quickly as possible. Another mystery I need to solve.

"So what do you think?" Aiden asks.

I take a pull from my beer like I'm pondering his question. In reality, all my brain cells have gone south.

"Don't tell me you're a Republican?" He shakes his head, grinning.

"A man never tells," I say.

He laughs at my response. Thank fuck, because I have no idea what we were talking about—or more to the point, what *he* was talking about.

"What's going on over here?" Mackenzie's mom, Katie, asks as she takes a seat next to her husband on the couch, across from me.

"Just talking. How long until the food's ready?" Aiden asks, wrapping his arm around her shoulder and fitting her into his side.

"The girls just finished setting up, so dinner shouldn't be much longer," she says.

Then her eyes land on me. I see them turn, calculating. She leans in, placing her elbows on top of her thighs.

"So . . . tell me about yourself, Wesley. Are you single?" she asks bluntly, catching me off guard.

I laugh.

"Katie . . ." Aiden sighs while she looks at him with mock innocence.

"What? I'm just curious."

"You're never just curious." He shakes his head at her.

"Well, this time I *am* just curious," she states before looking at me again. "So? Are you single, Wesley?"

I answer immediately in the affirmative, and her hands rub together like a villain who's plotting her next move to take over the world.

"Do you like baseball?" she continues, eyes twinkling.

"Yeah, I like baseball. But I'm more of a football man."

"Our daughter Mackenzie *loves* baseball."

"Does she?" I ask, tucking that tidbit of information away.

"Oh yeah. She has season tickets for the Mets. She never misses a game," she says. She looks past my shoulder and shouts across the room, "Mac! Come over here, honey!"

Turning my head, I watch a wide-eyed Mackenzie walk our way, looking like she wants the ground to open up and swallow her.

"Mom . . . ?" Mackenzie says once she's close.

I notice the drink in her hand and wonder if it's got alcohol in it. Then I move my eyes to her flat stomach. I've never once in my thirty-three years not worn a condom, but with her I didn't even think about it. My only thought was to get inside her as quickly as possible. Now this woman whom I barely know, whom I can't get off my mind, could be carrying my child. That idea fills me with something I don't understand . . . all I know is it isn't a bad something.

"I was just telling Wesley here that you have season tickets to the Mets. Maybe you can take him to a game sometime?" Katie suggests.

Mackenzie's body jolts at her mother's statement.

"I . . ." Mackenzie skates her eyes past me, and she quickly shakes her head. "It's not baseball season, Mom."

"Oh." Katie frowns, apparently unhappy with her plan being shot down. "Well, when *does* it start back up?"

"Not until April."

"Right. Then you will just have to take him to a game in April." She smiles at Mackenzie, then tips her head to the side. She looks at me as I roll my shoulder subconsciously. "Are you okay?"

"Old wound. It acts up from time to time," I say.

Her eyes soften before she looks up at her daughter with pride.

"Mac is a massage therapist. Maybe you can go see her at her office sometime. People say she has magic hands," Katie says.

Mac coughs and Aiden sighs.

I feel my lips twitch. Of course it's on the tip of my tongue to say that I know *exactly* how magical her hands are—from experience—but I hold the comment in.

"I might just do that." I take another pull from my beer as Mackenzie's eyes bore a hole into the side of my head.

I tip my head back and watch her swallow as heat flares between us. "Where's your office?"

Seeing her lick her bottom lip, I wonder if she's even going to tell me. I feel myself relax when she gives me the address. Tucking that information away in a box marked with her name in my head, a plan starts to formulate in my mind. There is obviously some serious chemistry between us. I know that from the looks she's been giving me. She feels it, too, so why the hell is she fighting it?

"That's great." Katie stands up, having no idea that she's just given me another chance with her daughter.

I promise myself then and there that if she runs the next time, I'll let her go. I know I'm lying to myself.

"Mom . . . ," Mackenzie says, but Katie ignores her while wrapping an arm through hers.

"Come on, honey. Let's go finish putting everything out on the table so we can feed these guys." She leads Mackenzie away, talking quietly.

I can't hear what they're saying, but I see Mackenzie's shoulders tense as her mom leads her to the door—and out of Levi's apartment. Probably to her sister's, across the hall.

"My wife is a nut. She means well, but she's a nut." Aiden shakes his head. Grinning at his comment, I take another pull from my beer. "I'm going to head on over to Fawn's place and see if they need any help." He stands, and I stand along with him.

"I'll join you."

Smiling, he pats my shoulder before leading the way across the hall. Most everyone has already gathered around the table when we get there, so I take a seat next to Levi—and directly across from Mackenzie, who is doing her best to avoid looking at me. While I study her, my hand clenches into a fist. I have to work to keep myself from touching her. To keep myself from forcing her to look at me. To make her acknowledge that there is something between us.

"You good, man?" Levi questions.

I pull my eyes from Mackenzie to look at him. "Yeah."

"Good."

He nudges my shoulder with his before leaning over to Fawn, who is sitting next to him. He whispers something in her ear that makes her smile. Pulling my eyes from them, I look at Mackenzie and find her eyes already on me. There are a million emotions playing behind her gaze. The moment is broken when her little sister takes a seat next to her and says something that makes her laugh. Seeing her smile, I know I want to see that smile again—only directed at me.

~

Parking down the block from Mackenzie's office four days later, I get out and pay the meter before heading toward the building. When I looked up Soothe Your Soul, the name of her practice, I found out that it was actually in an apartment building with a few other small businesses—all located on the first floor.

The rest of Thanksgiving dinner was interesting, to say the least. Levi's sister-in-law kept bringing up his ex, which in turn pissed everyone off. Fawn, who I could tell was hurt by the conversation, got up in the middle of dinner. She took her sisters with her, and they didn't come back for a long time. So long that I wondered if they'd come back at all. When they did return, Fawn wasn't with them, so Levi left in search of her. After he left, I decided that I would head home, too.

I swear I saw disappointment in Mackenzie's eyes when I told her and her family goodbye, but I knew not to get my hopes up. That doesn't mean they weren't. The need to see her again has been clawing at my gut since then.

I press the button next to the nameplate for her office, and the door buzzes. The lock clicks. I pull the door open and look around to see if there is a camera that will announce to her who has arrived. I don't see one—and that bothers me more than it probably should. The idea of her being alone and just letting anyone inside causes the caveman who's taken residence in me since meeting her to rear his ugly head.

Until I met her, I had never experienced possessiveness before. I had never understood the need to claim someone, to mark or brand them. Yet that is exactly what I want to do with her.

When I reach her office, I find the door open. She's sitting at her desk with her hair up in a ponytail, and her face is makeup-free. She has a Chinese-takeout container in front of her, and her eyes are on the computer. She looks beautiful. More beautiful than the night I met her, when she was dressed up and wearing makeup.

"Hey," I say.

Her head whirls around, and her eyes widen when she hears my voice.

"You . . . you're here."

"I was in the neighborhood." I shrug, knowing she'll catch on to the fact that I'm using the same lame excuse she did when I found her outside my door attempting to leave me a note. "Do you have any openings?"

For a long moment, she does nothing but stare at me like she can't believe that I'm standing in front of her.

"Mackenzie?" I take a step toward her, and she blinks.

"You . . ." She wiggles her head, causing her ponytail to move from side to side and to slide along her neck. "You want a massage?"

"Your mom suggested it might help me," I remind her.

She rolls her eyes as her lips lift into a small smile. "My mom is insane."

"A little," I agree. I ask my question again. "Do you have any time available today?"

She nibbles her bottom lip, studying me before answering. "My next client isn't scheduled to be here for another hour and a half."

"I'm sure we can make that work," I reply, feeling satisfaction when her eyes flash with desire and her nipples pebble under the thin top she has on.

"I . . . um . . ." She looks around. "You just need to fill out this paperwork." She picks up a clipboard and shoves it my way without looking at me. "I'll get everything set up, then come back out to get you."

I don't get a chance to reply before she takes off. I sit and fill out the paperwork as I was told. She comes back out a few minutes later and takes the clipboard from me. Tucking my hands into the front pockets of my jeans, I watch as she reads over everything quickly.

She sets the clipboard on top of the desk, then shuts and locks the door.

"Do you always lock the door when you have a client?" I ask as she looks up at me.

"Yes. If I'm with a client, the door is always locked. That way no one can just walk in while I'm working," she states.

I want to ask her about the fact that she buzzed me in without knowing who I was, but I can tell by the shortness in her tone that she wouldn't appreciate me questioning her right now.

"If you'll follow me." She scoots around me, and I follow her down a very short hall and into a dimly lit room where soft music is playing in the background.

The walls are a light blue, almost white. The color goes well with the pictures of the ocean she has hung on the walls. Pulling in a lungful of air, I realize the room smells like her—like lavender and vanilla.

"I'll give you a few minutes to get undressed and under the covers." She points at the massage bed in the middle of the room. It's covered in white sheets. "Just shout when you're ready for me."

"Don't leave on my account." I smile and toss my jacket on the chair in the corner of the room.

"This is my *job*." The words are breathy, giving away the desire she's feeling.

I use that to my advantage as I strip off my shirt.

"I take my job seriously."

"As you should." I nod in agreement, then kick off my sneakers and strip out of my jeans. "Should I leave them on, or lose them?" I question with my thumbs in the waistband of my boxers.

Her tongue wets her bottom lip, causing it to glisten—and my cock to throb.

"Leave them on."

"All right." I remove my fingers. "How do you want me?"

At my question, her eyes flare. She quickly schools her features and crosses her arms over her chest.

"On your stomach," she instructs.

Turning my back to her, I get onto the table and lie down on my stomach, cursing my hard-on when my weight presses it into the unyielding mattress. Resting my face in the cradle at the top of the bed, a million fantasies play out in my mind as I wait for the first touch from her hands.

When I hear her feet pad across the carpet and get closer, my body fills with anticipation. I hear her sharp inhale as her finger touches one of my scars.

"What are these from?"

"Gunshot," I say quietly, knowing she's looking at the three small scars on my right shoulder. I was shot during a drug bust gone bad.

"I didn't notice them before."

"You were a little preoccupied," I remind her, trying to lighten the mood.

She doesn't laugh or reply at all.

Feeling a drop of wet hit my back a moment later, my eyes tighten. Fuck.

I sit up and take her into my arms without thinking. I hold her against me as she cries, overwhelmed that she's upset over me.

"I'm sorry." She pulls away before I'm ready to let her go, ducking her head and wiping the wet from her cheeks. "I don't know what's wrong with me."

"I'm not going to complain that you let me hold you," I say.

Her eyes meet mine.

"How did it happen?" she asks.

I ignore the question, just like I've been ignoring the constant pain in my chest since I moved away from Seattle and to New York City.

"It's not important. Let's get started," I say, trying to keep the bite out of my tone. I know I don't succeed in that endeavor, because she flinches. "Sorr—"

"You're right." She cuts me off and looks away from me, making me want to kick my own ass around the room. "We should get started. My next client will be here soon."

Without a word, I move back to my stomach and close my eyes. Feeling her oil-covered hands slip across my back makes it almost impossible to relax. I want to apologize for being harsh and for shutting her down when she was obviously only concerned for me, but I can't get the words out. I've never opened up to anyone. I can't imagine that Mackenzie wants my burdens dragging her down.

"I was arrested once," she says out of the blue minutes later.

All the muscles that had started to relax tighten again, but she ignores my reaction and continues talking while gliding her hands across my skin.

"It was stupid, really. I skipped school one day and went to the park to hang out with a group of friends. We were all just being kids, not doing anything bad, but we were having fun. So much fun that I thought the moment should be recorded for history's sake. Like an idiot, I carved my full name and the date plus 'Peace, love, and happiness' into the top of one of the wooden tables in the park."

She laughs softly, and I smile at the sound.

"Two cops showed up at my house a few weeks later, asking where I was on that date. At first, I had no idea what date they were referring to, but that didn't last long. They had photos of my handiwork. Those made it perfectly clear that they knew where I had been. My dad, as you can imagine, was not impressed that his daughter had skipped school to deface public property. So he told the officers to arrest me."

"Your *dad* had you arrested?" I ask, incredulous, through a smile.

She laughs. "Yes, and that day I had the privilege of sitting in a jail cell for a few hours before my mom found out what happened and came to get me out."

"Was she pissed?"

"Pissed isn't even close to what she was. The minute I saw how mad she was, I begged one of the officers to keep me locked up. I had never heard her screech so loud in my life. Thankfully, I haven't heard that god-awful noise since then."

I can hear the smile in her voice, so I tip my head to the side to get a look at her face. Christ, she's beautiful. Seeing the smile she's wearing causes my breath to freeze in my lungs and my chest to ache.

"Needless to say, I never skipped school again—or defaced public property."

"Was that the only time you've been in trouble with the law?"

"No . . . that's just the only time I was arrested." She smirks, and my stomach muscles tighten while my cock starts to come back to life.

"Tell me." I roll to my back so that I can see her face as she talks.

Her hands lift away; then she makes some kind of internal decision and puts them on me again, beginning to massage my pecs and shoulders.

"On my twenty-first birthday, my friends thought it would be smart for me to start drinking at a legal age by ingesting tequila."

"Christ."

"Yeah, that about sums it up. That night, I ended up shirtless in Times Square, singing 'I'm a Little Teapot,'" she says.

My hands flex at my sides at the idea of anyone seeing her the way I have. God, what the hell is she doing to me?

"Thankfully, the officer who got the call about a girl singing and running around topless in Times Square took pity on me when I puked all over him. Instead of arresting me like he could have, he made my friends take me home. He followed us all the way there, then gave us a warning that the next time we wouldn't get off so easy."

"You got lucky."

"Believe me, I know. That is also the last time I ever drank tequila. Now if I even get a whiff of the stuff, my stomach turns and I find myself running for the nearest bathroom."

"I hate hot dogs," I tell her, wanting to share something about myself. I feel the need to, even if it's about something stupid.

"You hate hot dogs?"

"I can't stand them. When I was six, my parents got divorced."

"I'm sorry." Her hands go still and her soft eyes meet mine, causing something in my chest to get tight.

"Don't be. Some people are better apart. Believe me, my parents are those people."

"Is that why you hate hot dogs?"

"No," I laugh. "My dad took me for the summer the first year after they divorced, and he had no idea how to cook. So we had hot dogs at every meal. Hot dogs and eggs, hot dogs and mac and cheese, hot dogs in spaghetti. I swear, if someone would have drawn my blood after that summer, my cholesterol at six years old would have been through the roof."

"Poor kid."

"Yeah. Since then, I can't even look at a hot dog without wanting to get sick."

"That sucks. There is nothing better than sitting out under the sun at Mets stadium, drinking a beer, and eating a hot dog while watching a game."

"I'll have to take your word for that, gorgeous. I might drink a beer, but you will never see me eating a hot dog."

I notice how her pupils dilate when I say the word *gorgeous*.

Just when I think I'm getting somewhere, she quickly looks away.

"You should flip back to your stomach so I can finish working on your back."

"All right." I roll to my stomach, and for the next half hour we are both completely silent. She works my muscles from my shoulders to my calves. I don't fall asleep even though my eyes get heavy. I want to stay awake the whole time so I can soak in the feeling of her touch, the way her hands glide over my body. I try to memorize every single second since I'm not sure when her hands will be on me again.

"All done," she says softly when a chime sounds in the room.

I lean up on an elbow.

"I'll let you get dressed. Just come out when you're ready."

Even though a part of me knows that the smart thing to do would be to let her walk away and come to me if that's what she wants, I know I can't do it. I want *her*, and I want to figure out why she keeps acting like she doesn't want me, too. I can see it in her eyes and by the way her body reacts to me. She does.

Taking her hand before she's out of reach, I sit up on the side of the bed. "Go out with me tonight." I hate how vulnerable I sound to my own ears.

"Go out with you?" she repeats.

I wonder why the hell she can't seem to believe that I want to spend time with her.

"Have dinner with me." I pull her a step closer.

Her bottom lip disappears between her teeth before she releases it and gives me a nod.

"If that's a yes, I'm going to need to hear you say the word . . ."

"Yes."

"Good." I rub my thumb over the pulse at her wrist and feel it beating hard. "I'll pick you up at your place at six."

"I'll meet you at the restaurant."

I want to insist on picking her up, but I can tell by the look in her eyes that she won't give in. Knowing I need to pick my battles right now, I don't fight her to get my way.

"All right, we'll meet at the restaurant," I agree. I give her the name of the place I have in mind before she leaves the room.

Once I'm dressed, I head out into the main part of the office and find her laughing with a guy—not just any guy, a good-looking guy who is standing way too damn close.

I clear my throat and watch as her head swings my way. My instinct is to puff up my chest when the guy looks me over, sizing me up.

"Wesley, this is my friend Edward. Edward, this is Wesley."

I take the guy in. He's tall, with the body of an athlete. His hair is short and his jaw is clean, which fits with the suit he has on. He looks like a sleazy banker.

"Nice to meet you."

Edward lifts his chin, and I do the same in return before looking at Mackenzie. I move toward her with purpose, needing and wanting to stake my claim on her in some way.

"See you tonight," I tell her as I drop a kiss on her cheek.

I feel her breath come out in a puff across my ear. I lean back, searching her gaze and feeling self-satisfied when I see that her eyelids have lowered and her face has gotten soft.

"Yeah, I'll see you tonight," she whispers.

I swear it takes everything in me to leave her there with another man. It kills me a little when I hear her office door shut and lock behind me once I'm in the hall. Then I remind myself that she's not mine. That still doesn't stop the caveman in my head from growling. *Mine.*

Chapter 4

COMPLICATED

MAC

Stripping out of my clothes, I take a seat on the side of my bed in my tank top and panties. I scratch my hands down my face, thinking about tonight. I have a date. Not only do I have a date, but I have a date with Wesley. I couldn't believe it when I looked up and found him standing in my doorway this afternoon wearing jeans, his leather jacket, and boots. His hair was mussed like he had run his hand through it a few dozen times. I had thought that I was imagining him since I had just taken his number out of my desk and dialed it—but I hung up before I pressed the last number. It wasn't until he said my name and stepped toward me that I realized he was really there.

Flopping back onto my bed, I close my eyes. I think about the scars on his shoulder and his tortured expression when I asked about them. There was something about it that made me want to crawl into his lap and hold him, to tell him that it would be okay. I don't know what happened to him, but I know that whatever it was still affects him. He shut down completely when I brought it up. That stung. I didn't know how to react or what to say, so I pulled away in response.

Only that wasn't working for me, either. I didn't like the distance or weird energy that settled over us like a wet blanket just then, which is why I told him about being arrested when I was younger. I wanted to make him smile or, better yet, laugh. I didn't expect him to open up to me and tell me about a piece of his childhood in return, but he did. That made the connection I feel with him grow a little more. It also made it easy for me to agree to go out with him. Well, that and the fact that he looks at me like I'm already his.

At that thought, my skin tingles and my body hums. Intellectually, I know I shouldn't find it as hot as I do that he seems so possessive about me, but my body has other ideas. There is something powerful in knowing that I can cause those kinds of emotions. When he saw me talking to Edward, I thought for a moment that he was going to storm across the room, pick me up, toss me over his shoulder, and carry me away with him.

I swallow, and hard anxiety hits the pit of my stomach. Reality crashes down around me like a ton of bricks. The last time I thought I had a connection with someone, I was very, very wrong. Am I just as wrong this time around? I need to stop thinking of this thing between us in terms of something serious. I should just think of it as a little bit of fun. No-strings-attached fun that won't lead to me being broken-hearted. I shouldn't assume anything more. We are just two people who are attracted to each other and who have over-the-top, out-of-this-world chemistry.

"Mac?" Libby's singsong hello floats from the living room, cutting into my wayward thoughts.

I sit up on the side of the bed.

"I'm in the bedroom!" I shout back, wondering why it's necessary to inform her of that—our apartment is less than five hundred square feet. She would have found me eventually, even without looking.

"What's up, sister dearest?" She comes into the room with her long, dark hair tied up into a neat bun and her makeup done perfectly.

"Nothing much," I answer, watching her dump her purse on her twin bed, which is directly across from mine.

She starts stripping out of her slacks and fitted blouse—something that she always does the moment she gets home, which makes me wonder why she bothers wearing things that are obviously so uncomfortable. "Do you feel like ordering a pizza and watching a horror flick?" She turns to look at me once she has on her baggy sweats and an even baggier T-shirt.

"I'm actually going out in a bit. I'm meeting a friend for dinner."

"Oh, can I come?"

Oh lord. How do I answer that? Libby often comes out with me when I'm meeting friends, so I know if I tell her she can't come, she will have a million questions for me—questions I'm not ready to answer.

"Never mind. I don't feel like getting dressed again," she says as she heads toward the bathroom, taking her hair out of the bun as she goes.

Sighing in relief, I play it off like I'm disappointed when she comes back out. "Are you sure?"

"Yeah, it's freezing out. They said it's going to snow. I don't want to be stuck outside wearing heels if it's snowing."

"You could just wear regular shoes . . ." I point out the obvious.

She rolls her eyes at me, making me smile. I don't know how Libby does it, but she manages to wear heels even though she's on her feet all day doing makeup for the who's who of New York City at the posh upscale boutique where she works.

"I own one pair of rain boots and one pair of sneakers—and they are both still brand new and in the box they came in." She lies down on her bed, then rolls her head toward me. Her eyes scan my face. "Are you okay?"

"Yep," I say. Maybe I answered a little too quickly, because her eyes narrow. She lifts herself up on an elbow and rests her head in her hand.

"You've been weird since before Thanksgiving. What's going on?"

There is a six-foot-two gorgeous, giant man taking up my every waking thought, I think but don't say.

"Nothing's wrong. Just a little tired." I shrug one shoulder.

"Hmm." She studies me like a speck of dirt under a microscope.

Needing to avoid the interrogation I feel coming, I stand and head for the bathroom.

"So tell me about Wesley."

Dammit! I pause and turn to look at her over my shoulder. "Wesley?" I feign ignorance.

She huffs out a breath. "Yeah, Levi's hot friend Wesley. How do you know him?"

Bunching my eyebrows together to give her the full effect I ask, "*Know* him?"

"You know what? Never mind." She sits up, then pushes herself off the bed and starts for the door, grumbling as she goes.

"Libby . . ."

"No." She shakes her head, turning to face me. "You, me, and Fawn used to be close. We used to tell one another everything. Now I feel like everything is some big secret. It's annoying."

"It's complicated," I admit.

She frowns. "Life is always complicated. That's what family is for—to help you uncomplicate things, to talk things out, and to be there," she says. Before I can open my mouth to reply, she continues. "All I'm saying is if you guys don't want to share what's going on in your lives, then I won't be sharing what's going on in mine." With that parting shot, she leaves me standing in our bedroom, feeling two feet tall and riddled with guilt for not opening up to her.

I should tell her and Fawn about what's happened between Wesley and me. But the idea of doing that and having to risk seeing the pity in their eyes later if things don't work out leaves me feeling torn. I hate that they witnessed my crush on Edward, that they saw firsthand how desperately I tried to get him to see me, how I went out of my way to spend time with him. I looked like an idiot, pining over a guy who was never more than a friend, who never led me to believe that we *could* be more. I'm supposed to be the oldest one, the experienced one. Instead, I'm the one who wasted two years of her life on a crush. A crush on a guy I now feel nothing for. How crazy is that?

When Edward came to my office today, I didn't get butterflies like the ones I get whenever I see Wesley. My pulse didn't kick into overdrive. My palms didn't itch to touch him. My mind didn't scream at him to kiss me. I really don't remember *any* of those things ever happening before when I was around Edward. In fact, in hindsight I have no idea what I saw in him in the first place.

I run my hands down my face, willing myself to give up on figuring that out right now. I head for the bathroom, where I get in the bathtub and try not to think about what will happen tonight. Not that it matters.

~

Two hours later, I'm sitting in a cab and watching the city go by in a flash of dazzling lights. The glow is accentuated by the snow that is steadily falling from the night sky. When I checked the weather report before I left home, it said that New York City was expected to get at least two inches of the white stuff by morning. There will be a few more flurries tomorrow afternoon, which means work will most likely be slow. A lot of my clients are older and don't like going out in the snow.

"Here you are." My cab driver pulls me out of my thoughts as he comes to a stop. The steady hum of nervous energy I've been feeling all evening expands through every inch of me.

After running my credit card through the machine on the backseat, I put my hand on the door handle. I don't have a chance to push it open before it's opened for me. I look up.

Wesley is there, holding out his hand. I feel a sudden rush of excitement as our eyes lock and I place my hand in his.

"Thank you." I smile as I step out onto the street, then hiss out a breath when my boot catches on a crack in the ground and I stumble into him.

"I got you." He catches me before I can fall and pulls me against him, holding me there. He shuts the cab door and leads us to the sidewalk.

"Thanks." I look up at him as the cab pulls away and swallow when I see the look in his eyes.

He cups my jaw with his warm hand, and his thumb presses into my bottom lip.

"I've been thinking about kissing you all day."

"You have?"

"Oh yeah." He tips his head down until our mouths are a mere centimeter apart. "All goddamn day," he rumbles.

My stomach clenches while my hands hold on to his coat. I feel his sides tighten in response.

"Wesley?" I call softly after a moment.

His forehead touches mine. "Yeah?"

"*Are* you going to kiss me?" I ask breathlessly.

He growls right before he captures my mouth with a kiss that makes me so light-headed, I see stars.

When his teeth nibble my bottom lip as he pulls away, my body quivers and the space between my legs tingles.

"Gorgeous."

"Hmm?" I slowly open my eyes and find him looking down at me and smiling.

"As much as I want to keep kissing you, we have a reservation."

"Oh . . ." I look around, then shake my head to try and clear my lust-fogged mind. "Right," I say.

His laughing lips touch my forehead. Taking my hand, he leads me toward a restaurant at the end of the block. The place is really nice, and its dim lighting makes the large room feel intimate. Small booths line the walls, and round tables dot the middle of the space. It's all white tablecloths and fancy folded napkins and gleaming place settings. As I look around, I feel like I should have looked up the restaurant online to check the dress code.

"Are you okay?"

"Um . . ." I look around again before looking up at him. "I think I might be underdressed for this restaurant," I admit.

His eyes roam my face, then the thick scarf wrapped around my neck, and move down over my long, black wool coat. It hits me midthigh, covering my sweater and jeans.

"You look beautiful."

I want to kiss him for the easy way he made that compliment, but I don't. I shake my head instead and squeeze his hand. "I have on a sweater and jeans."

"It's okay. There isn't a dress code here," he says.

Judging by the way everyone else in the restaurant is dressed, I have to disagree with him. They might not have a formal dress code, but I have no doubt they will frown at my choice of clothing the minute I take off my coat.

"What are you doing?" I ask when he starts to lead me back toward the door we just entered moments before.

"I don't want you to be uncomfortable, and I can tell that you are."

"But you made a reservation."

"Yeah, and I can make another one another time." He opens the door, leading me back outside.

"Are you sure?"

He stops on the sidewalk, turns me in his arms to face him, and dips his face toward mine until we are eye to eye. "Tonight is just about us spending time together, us getting to know each other. I don't care where we are or what we're doing as long as you're with me."

I look into his eyes. I know I could definitely fall for this guy.

"Now, where are we going? It's your choice."

It's on the tip of my tongue to tell him we should go back to his place, but I know the smart thing to do is to get to know each other outside of his bedroom.

"Do you like pizza?" At my question, his eyebrows shoot up, and his hold on me tightens. I don't know what that response means. "It's just that I'm dressed for pizza, and there is a really great pizza spot not far from here—"

"Pizza it is!" He cuts me off before I can blabber anything else. "Is it close enough to walk to in the cold, or do we need to get in a cab?"

"We can walk," I say softly.

He brushes his mouth over mine, then takes my hand in his. "Lead the way."

We go three blocks down, to Tony's. I listen to him tell me about the rest of his day as I soak in the feeling of his hand holding mine. His towering presence at my side makes me feel protected. I know if something were to happen, he would do whatever he had to do in order to make sure I was okay. I have never felt that before with any-one. When we finally reach the restaurant and step inside, I expect to be greeted by Tony, like always. He's not there, which surprises me since he's always behind the long counter laughing with customers or his employees.

"What kind of pizza do you like?" Wesley asks, pulling my atten-tion back to him.

I shrug. "Anything with meat on it."

"My kind of girl!" He smiles, and my heart flips. "Do you want to grab us a booth while I place our order?" he asks, looking around the packed restaurant.

"Sure."

I release his hand and head toward the back just as a couple leaves one of the tables. Tonight, like most nights at Tony's, seating is a rare commodity. It's not a fancy place, but it doesn't have to be—the pizza brings people from all over Manhattan.

Sliding into the empty table, I rub my freezing hands together and blow on my fingers while I watch Wesley place our order. Feeling more at ease, I slip off my coat and set it on the bench next to me, then unwrap the scarf from around my neck and drop it on top of the coat. This place is definitely more my style. Okay, really this place is like a second home to me. Libby and I spend a lot of time here together because pizza is one of the few things we can have without blowing our monthly budgets. Over time, we've become close to Tony and his wife. We've also gotten to know his son, Antonio, who helped out his dad after he got out of the military and still does now, whenever he isn't working as a firefighter.

"Mac!" I turn my head when I hear my name. I smile at Antonio when he comes over to greet me with a hug.

"Hey, how are things?" I ask when he lets me go.

"I'm guessing you didn't hear?" he says, taking a seat across from me.

I notice the exhaustion and worry in his eyes, which puts me on guard. "Hear what?"

"My dad had a heart attack."

"What?" My heart splits open just thinking about Tony—happy, smiling Tony—in the hospital.

"Yeah." He runs a hand through his hair. "He had to have surgery, and he's been in the hospital for a couple days now. They are getting ready to move him to a nursing home to recover and get physical therapy."

"Oh my god." I reach over and take his hand. "I'm so sorry. I had no idea."

"Mom's a mess, which is probably why she didn't tell you. She's been staying with him as much as she can and working here when she's not."

"What can I do to help?" I ask immediately.

He smiles softly, and I realize then just how good-looking he is. He's so not my type—my type seems to be just Wesley—but he is attractive. Why didn't I see that before?

"Do you know how to make pizza?" He laughs, but I can tell he's serious.

"I don't, but I can learn. Libby can also help out."

"Libby the never-a-hair-out-of-place, high-heel-wearing princess?" He snorts.

I narrow my eyes at him. "You'd be surprised. She's a hard worker, and she worked at the pizza place by our house when she was in high school," I say to defend her, but he shakes his head.

"No, thanks." He waves the idea away.

I want to ask him why not, but I don't have a chance. A shadow envelops our table, and I tip my head back to find Wesley looking down at us—or more like glowering down at the man across from me.

"Can I help you?" Antonio asks.

Wesley's jaw shifts.

"Ant, this is my . . ."

"Boyfriend." He sticks out a hand toward Antonio. "Wesley."

"Oh?" Antonio looks from Wesley to me. "Seems like we both have news."

"Um . . ." I look up at Wesley, half wanting to kick him and half wanting to tear off his clothes. I don't know how he is able to make me feel so conflicted.

"Nice to meet you." Antonio stands and shakes his hand. "Keep an eye on her—she's a wild card. I think it has something to do with the red hair." He smirks, and Wesley grunts something I can't make out before Antonio leans over to kiss my cheek. "I'm happy for you, kid. It's about damn time."

"Thanks, I think," I mumble as he laughs and walks away.

Sensing Wesley slide into the booth, I keep my eyes off him. I'm not sure what to say.

"How many other men are you friends with?"

"Pardon?" I look at him, slightly appalled at his question.

He sits forward. "Edward. Antonio. Who else is there?"

"Is that a question you really want me to answer?" I ask only because he already looks annoyed.

"I'm guessing by that response my answer is going to be no."

"I've always had more male friends than female." I shrug.

"Why?"

"I find men to be more easygoing. I don't have to worry about what they are thinking, or that they'll talk about me behind my back. It's simple with men. Give them a beer and a game and they're happy. Women are a whole different world."

"Have you ever had a relationship with any of your male friends?" he asks, making me squirm in my seat. "Is that a yes?"

"No, I . . . I had a crush on one of them, but nothing ever happened."

"Who?"

"I'm not telling you."

"Who?" he repeats quietly.

"You're really annoying," I huff out.

His eyes narrow. "That's not an answer."

"Edward." I roll my eyes. "Are you happy now? I had a crush on him, but he never even knew about it. He never saw me as anything more than a friend. Really, I don't know what I saw in him to begin with."

"The guy from today? Your next appointment?" He sits back in the seat, crossing his arms over his chest.

"Yeah."

"Jesus," he curses.

I look up to find him rubbing his forehead. "What?"

"You touched him," he growls.

I feel my brows pull together. *"What?"*

"You touched him. You gave him a massage after me."

"Yeah, he's my *client*," I agree, wondering where he's going with this.

He shakes his head and grumbles, "Not anymore."

"Pardon?"

"He can't be your client anymore," he states, sitting forward and getting as close as he can with the table between us.

"Are you insane?" I hiss, pointing at him. "First of all, you do not *ever* get to tell me what to do. Second, you are a jerk for even thinking that I would be anything less than professional with the men and women I have as clients."

"I wasn't saying that."

"Yeah? Then what were you saying?"

"I don't like the idea of your hands on him while you're locked behind a closed door."

"Too bad," I mutter as I pick up my scarf and wrap it around my throat with an angry jerk.

"Where are you going?" he asks, looking panicked when he sees me slip on my coat.

"I'm leaving. Enjoy the pizza—it's the best in New York City." I stand and start to walk away, but he takes my hand, forcing me to stop and look at him.

"You're running again."

"Call it whatever you like." I tug my hand free and head for the door.

Out on the sidewalk, I rush as quickly as I can toward my block. I feel him hot on my heels as I go. As soon as I make it up to my apartment, I hear him enter the foyer behind me and follow me up the steps.

"Stop!" he pleads as I put my key in the door.

Everything in me fights the urge to listen to him.

"Please!" His body presses into my back, his hand slides around my waist, and his lips touch my neck as he speaks. "I'm sorry. I shouldn't have told you who you could or could not have as clients."

"No, you shouldn't have."

"Can you please look at me?" he asks.

I shudder as I slowly turn around to face him, wondering vaguely if Miss Ina is downstairs listening to this conversation take place. I have no doubt that, if she is, I'll get an earful tomorrow.

"This is new to me." He takes my face between his hands. "I've never felt the way you make me feel. You make me crazy. The idea of someone else touching you—or you touching them—makes me see red."

"Do you know how insane that is?" I ask while asking myself how insane *I* am for enjoying his reaction.

"I do." He shakes his head and runs his fingers through his hair. "Believe me, I know. And I'm sorry."

"You can't tell me what to do, Wesley. And you can *never* tell me how I should do my job, or who I can have as clients or friends. That is a deal breaker for me. I like you, and for some insane reason I like that you feel as jealous as you do about me, but that can never spill over into my work life or erode the friendships I've had for years."

"I know," he agrees, placing one hand on the door above my head and the other on my hip while dipping his face close to mine.

I swallow, then lower my eyes so I won't have to look at him when I say what I'm about to. "I think we should just slow this down a little," I whisper, peeking up at him through my lashes. "This thing between us has been very intense from the beginning. M-maybe we need to take a step back," I say, hating the very idea of doing that.

"Do you want that?" he asks. I try to force myself to say yes or to nod, but I can't do it.

Pulling my body deeper into his, he lowers his face until we are eye to eye. "Do you really want us to take a step back?"

No! my mind screams as he trails hot kisses across my cheek and toward my ear.

"Invite me in so I can remind you of why you want this," he murmurs.

My eyes slide closed.

When he pulls my hips into his and I feel his arousal between us, I whimper, "I can't. My sister's home, and I . . . I don't want her to find out about us."

"You don't want her to *find out* about us?" He steps back suddenly, like I burned him.

I realize what I said and how it sounded. Looking into his eyes and seeing the hurt there, I reach out to touch him. He backs up a step.

"I'm sorry. I didn't . . ." My apology dies in my throat when he turns and starts down the steps, taking them two at a time. "Please stop!" I shout at his back, but he doesn't. He doesn't even turn around as I try to catch up with him. "Wesley!" I stumble to a stop at the bottom of the steps and watch him disappear out the front door.

"Let him go, child."

I turn my head to find Miss Ina standing in her open doorway. "He'll calm down, and then you'll be able to talk to him," she says gently as her frail fingers wrap around mine and tears fill my eyes. "Men get like that from time to time. It's best you let them work through their anger."

"I messed up," I whisper.

Her fingers tighten. "It will be okay. Come have a cup of tea."

Wiping at the tears that are running down my cheeks, I shake my head. "Miss Ina, now's not a good time."

"Now is the best time." She tugs my hand, leaving me no choice but to follow her into her apartment.

Chapter 5

Under My Skin

Wesley

I don't want her to find out about us.

Those fucking words replay in my mind on a loop, tormenting me as I walk from Mackenzie's house toward mine. She doesn't want her sisters to know about us. That thought makes me want to break something. It also makes me wonder what's wrong with me. I know I could walk into any number of bars right now and leave with a woman of my choosing, and I can almost guarantee she would stick around until morning. Hell, she'd probably fucking make me breakfast in bed and ask when we could hang out again.

"This is your fault," I mutter under my breath as I glare at the vicinity of my dick. Since the moment he met Mackenzie, he's been fascinated with her. He's lost interest in everyone else.

Who the hell am I kidding? My mind has become solely focused on her, too. She's what I think about before I fall asleep at night and the first thing I think about in the morning. Maybe I should turn in my badge and start writing cards for Hallmark.

Tucking my hands into the front pocket of my coat, I duck my head. It's freezing, but the bite of cold is keeping me focused, keeping me from turning around and heading right back to her place—where I would undoubtedly make an even bigger fool of myself by tossing her over my shoulder, carrying her home with me, cuffing her to my bed, and forcing her to admit her feelings.

Grinding my teeth, I quicken my steps. When I finally make it to my block a little more than an hour and a half later, I'm soaking wet. I shuck off my jacket and kick off my boots by the door as soon as I open it so that I don't drag water and snow across the floor.

I pull in a deep breath and let it out slowly when I see a message from Mackenzie on my cell phone. I stare at my cell for a minute, then shake my head and turn it off. I should have learned my lesson the first time she took off on me—but I didn't. I should have realized that I'm not what she wants when she ran from me the *second* time we hooked up—but once again, I didn't. Now I know for certain that she doesn't want her family to know about me. I never thought I would be living a life where I would be someone's dirty little secret, but that is exactly what I am to her.

Grunting in disgust at myself, I head for the shower. I stand under the hot water until it runs cold, then get out and go to bed. I keep my phone off so that I'm not tempted to talk to her.

~

Pulling my bulletproof vest down over my head the next evening, I Velcro the sides and then put on my jacket. I need to get my head in the game and off Mackenzie. Mackenzie, who's called or texted at least a dozen times this morning to apologize. Mackenzie, whose last text said that she was now pissed at me for being pissed at her. That message shouldn't have made me smile, but it did.

Stop thinking about her . . . I need to get focused on what's about to go down.

This morning, Levi and I were finally able to procure a warrant for Juan Varges, a suspect in a missing-persons case we've been working on for the last three weeks. Two hours ago, I got word from an informant on where our suspect has been hiding out ever since the woman turned up missing. Varges is a known pimp with multiple homicides linked to his name. Unfortunately, until now, we haven't had any solid evidence that we could use against him. When you're a cop, going into any situation half-blind is dangerous. And when that situation involves a man with nothing to lose who is being backed into a corner, it could be deadly.

"What the hell is going on with you?"

Turning my head, I look at Levi. Since I moved to New York, he's been my only real friend. He's also one of the few people who knows why I moved here. I don't know what his reaction would be if I told him about Mackenzie and me.

"I know something's up, so let's get it out on the table before we go get our guy," he says, leaning against the side of his SUV after holstering his gun.

I shake my head. "I don't even know where to begin."

"The beginning is always a good place." He crosses his arms.

I let out a breath.

"I've been sleeping with Mackenzie." Saying the words out loud lifts a weight off my shoulders that I didn't even know was there.

A frown drags Levi's brows together.

"She doesn't want her sister to know about us."

"You've been sleeping with *Mackenzie*? As in Fawn's sister Mac?"

"Yeah." I slam the door and head toward the trunk, with Levi following.

"Dude." He runs his hand over his head. "When the hell did this start? Was it after you met her at Thanksgiving?"

"No. I met her at a bar a few days before that. She came home with me that night, then took off the next morning before I woke up, but she forgot her cell phone at my place. A few days later, she came by to get it, and we ended up in bed again. Trust me—I was *shocked* to see her at your place on Thanksgiving."

"I bet." He scrubs his hands against his face. "So . . . what's going on between you two now?"

"Nothing. She told me that she didn't want Libby to know about us."

"Ouch."

"Yeah." My jaw clenches when I think that she wants to keep us a secret.

"Maybe she didn't mean it the way you took it."

"I'm not sure there is another way to take it."

"I don't know, man. You met her parents. You saw just how crazy her mom is. Maybe she's afraid that if her sister knows about you two, she'll tell their mom, who'll start trying to influence how Mac is feeling."

"Maybe." I check my gun before holstering it under my arm. "All I know is that she's making me fucking crazy."

"Welcome to the club," he laughs.

I smirk at him. It wasn't long ago that he had come into work complaining about his new neighbor. His neighbor who is now his girlfriend. After seeing them together, how happy they are, and how obviously in love he is with her, I have no doubt that it won't be long before he'll put a ring on her finger.

"Have you spoken to her since then?" he asks.

I shake my head. "No, but she did send me a message letting me know that she's now pissed at me because I'm pissed at her," I tell him.

He smiles.

"As soon as we're done here, I say you go to her and figure out what's going on. Just ask why she doesn't want her sister to know about you."

I don't know what the hell I'm going to do. Last night, I was sure about letting her go. I thought I could find a way to get over whatever this is. But when I woke up this morning, I found myself thinking of her and wondering if she's okay, if she slept, if she was thinking about me the way I was thinking about her. Breaking it off would be impossible. She's burrowed under my skin in the short time I've known her. Now I need to figure out how to either get under hers or get over her.

"Are you ready?" I ask, needing to change the subject and my train of thought.

Mackenzie is exactly what I *don't* need to be thinking about right now.

"Yeah." Levi pulls himself off the bumper where he had taken a seat.

Folding the warrant for our suspect in half, I shove it in the inside pocket of my jacket and pull my cell phone out. Holding it in my hand, I wonder if I should wait to talk to Mackenzie face-to-face. I know I probably should, but the idea of going into this situation without hearing her voice doesn't sit well with me.

"Just call her, man. She and Libby were picking up Fawn to go out when you called to tell me that we finally got Varges."

"Where were they going?" I ask, not sure I want to know the answer. If he tells me they are out at some bar, I might lose my mind.

"Some art show in SoHo," he says.

My muscles relax. I see another police cruiser drive by and park down at the end of the block, behind the SWAT van. Time to go.

"Call her. Don't go into this situation without letting her know that you're thinking about her." He pats my shoulder, then walks off toward the other officers gathered at the end of the block.

I dial and put the phone to my ear. I clench my fist when my call goes to voice mail.

"I'll see you tonight," I growl before I hang up. I shove my phone back in my pocket.

As Levi and I follow SWAT into the building—and up the ten flights of stairs to Juan's girlfriend's apartment—adrenaline starts to course through my veins.

I used to live for this, for these moments of excitement. Now the unknown fills my belly with dread and makes me even more aware that there are lives on the line here. When we reach the stairwell on the tenth floor, I brace my back against the wall and wait for the signal from SWAT to say that they have entered the apartment and it's clear for Levi and me to go in. I close my eyes for a moment, say a silent prayer.

"Ready?" one of the SWAT officers asks, sticking his head into the stairwell a second later. Levi and I follow him down the hall toward the open apartment door. Upon entering, I do a quick scan of the room. There are two doors, both open. One leads to a bedroom, the other to a bathroom. The kitchen adjoins the living room. I walk in and see a TV on a glass stand, with a couch across from it. A woman who must be Juan's girlfriend is sitting with her hands on her lap. Juan lies on his belly on the floor with two SWAT officers to either side of him.

Pulling the warrant out of my pocket, I stride toward Juan's girl-friend but stop abruptly when she reaches down between her legs and pulls out something black. It takes a second for me to react and to yell, "Gun!"

As soon as the word leaves my mouth, all hell breaks loose. The officers holding Juan lose their hold on him as bullets start flying, which gives him just enough leeway to grab a weapon from under the entertainment unit. It feels like I'm watching him lift the gun in slow motion. I shout again, but it's too late. He takes the shot. Everything seems to stop as the bullet hits Levi, who goes down.

Not again, not again.

I breathe in through my nose and out through my mouth as I make my way across the floor on my hands and knees toward Levi. His back is to me. Once I'm close enough to touch him, I grab on to the collar of his jacket and drag him with me until we're both behind the couch.

Please be alive! I silently beg, rolling him onto his back.

His chest is rising and falling, but he's bleeding.

I yell over the sound of grunts and shouting. "We need an ambulance—now!"

I strip off my jacket and put it over his shoulder to put pressure on the entry wound.

"Fawn . . . ," he says as I add more pressure. "Call Fawn."

"I'll call her," I promise as his eyes slide closed. "Get a fucking ambulance!" I yell again as blood pools out from between my fingers.

There's too much blood—way too much blood. My stomach turns and my pulse thumps hard.

I can't do this. I can't do this again. I can't lose anyone else.

"Medical is on their way up now," one of the SWAT officers says as he gets down on his knees across from me. "Do you want me to take over?"

Shaking my head, I keep my eyes on my hands—they're covered in blood.

"Medic's here."

I lift my head and watch four EMTs come into the apartment, carrying a stretcher and bags with them.

"We got it," one of the female EMTs says.

But I don't move. I can't.

"You can't let him die." I swallow over the lump in my throat, and her hand covers mine.

"I promise we will take care of him, but you have to let us do our job." She gives me a reassuring smile.

I look from her back to Levi.

"Thank you." I stand back and watch them go to work on my partner, my friend.

Once they slow the bleeding and make sure he's stable, they lift the gurney up off the floor and start pushing him out of the apartment and into the hall. He doesn't look as pale as he was a few minutes ago, but his skin is still clammy, and his eyes won't stay open for longer than a few seconds.

"It will be okay, man." I follow him and the EMTs toward the elevators.

"Don't worry about me. Just call Fawn. Tell her I'll be okay."

"I'll tell her."

"Take my phone." He tries to reach for his cell, but one of the EMTs stops him as we all get in the elevator.

Reaching around the EMT—and ignoring the look she gives me—I take his phone and shove it into my pocket.

"I'll meet you at the hospital," I tell him when the elevator comes to a stop on the first floor.

"Just call Fawn."

"I'll call," I assure him.

I rub the back of my neck as I watch the EMTs put him into the ambulance parked at the curb, the lights flashing. Dropping my eyes to my boots, I tighten my fingers around his phone before putting it to my ear. I head for Levi's SUV, wishing I didn't have to make this call.

MAC

Holding Fawn's hand tightly, I watch Wesley pace at the end of the hall. Back and forth, back and forth, with his hands on his hips and his eyes on the swinging doors. When we arrived at the hospital, Wesley took my hand and led us up here, to a waiting area just outside the surgical unit. He said that Levi was stable when the ambulance left with him, and that the doctors assured him when he arrived that Levi would be okay. I know none of that information has really put Fawn's mind at ease.

When Wesley called Fawn and told her that Levi had been shot, I felt my heart crack open—because I knew that he had been with Levi. I knew in my gut that he could have been hurt as well. If something had happened to him, I would have hated myself for being an idiot. For trying to deny this thing between us. For constantly pushing him away these last few days, when I should have remembered how short life is.

"You should go to him," Fawn says.

I pull my gaze from Wesley to look at her tearstained face and worry-filled eyes. Over dinner earlier tonight, I had told her and Libby about Wesley. I had told them how we met and what had happened since then. They didn't think I was an idiot for liking him or thinking that he liked me—but they did think I was an idiot for hiding it.

"I will, when the doctors come out and tell us that Levi is doing okay." I squeeze her fingers.

She shakes her head. "Please go to him now." She closes her eyes, and pain fills my chest as I watch a tear fall down her cheek.

I know she didn't think that tonight would end up like this. That the same night she admitted to me and Libby she's in love with Levi, she almost lost him.

"Please." She opens her eyes. "Please."

With a jerky nod, I lean over and kiss her cheek. I stand and wipe my hand down the front of my slacks as I walk slowly toward Wesley.

Once I'm close enough to touch him, I reach out and place my hand on his back. I watch his body shudder. I don't even have time to prepare—he turns around and pulls me against his chest, holding me so tight that it's almost hard to breathe. Squeezing my eyes closed, I rest my ear over his heart and listen to it pound behind his rib cage.

"I'm sorry, I . . . I'm so, so sorry," I whisper, holding him as tight as I can.

He presses his face into my neck. His pain is palpable, and I know that what happened tonight has brought whatever hurt him in his past back to the present.

"It's going to be okay." I turn my head and press a kiss over his heart.

His arms tighten before he lets me go and takes a step back, shoving his hands in the front pocket of his jeans.

"Go be with your sisters."

"I—"

"Go. Fawn needs you." He jerks his chin toward Fawn as he takes another step back. Those few feet between us feel like thousands of miles. "Go!" he says gruffly.

My heart lurches when he turns his back on me. I want to refuse to go. I want to wrap my arms around him and hold him, but I can tell by the set of his shoulders that he doesn't want me. Biting the inside of my cheek, I try and fight back the pain in my chest. I take my seat next to Fawn again, who is now resting her head on Libby's shoulder with her eyes closed.

"It will be okay," Libby says.

I know she's talking to me, but I don't acknowledge her comment because my heart is splintering into a million pieces inside my chest. I can only sit there in a daze and stare at Wesley's back.

Finally, the doctors come out and tell us that Levi is doing okay.

~

"Do you want more?" Libby asks, holding out a bag of M&M's in my direction. My stomach revolts against the offer by gurgling.

Three hours ago, after the doctor came out to tell us that Levi was in his own room and Fawn followed him back, Wesley left to talk to the other officers who had also been waiting for word on Levi. Not long after that, our parents showed up, and Levi's family arrived. Libby and I have been hanging out in here in the waiting room since.

"So, do you?" Libby jiggles the bag of M&M's in front of my face.

"No, thanks." I shake my head.

"Your loss." She shoves another handful into her mouth before looking at me once more. "Are you going to talk to Wesley after we leave here?"

"I don't know. I really think I ruined things between us," I admit while wrapping my arms around my middle. "I . . . I hurt him. I honestly didn't think that after the way we started that he would want anything more than one night—despite him showing me otherwise time and again. I've been so afraid to put myself out there with him that I pushed him away before he could do it first."

"You should have talked to me and Fawn before Thanksgiving. If you had, none of this would have happened! We could have saved you from all this drama. We could have told you that you were being ridiculous and helped you to remember that any guy would be lucky to have you," she says.

I feel my face get soft. "You're probably right."

"I'm always right."

"Whatever." I shake my head.

She gets up and walks across the empty waiting room to the vending machine. She puts in a dollar, then presses the buttons for a soda.

"All I'm saying is that you should talk to him. Tell him the truth about what happened. Tell him that you were worried that he wouldn't want you, and scared that you would end up hurt."

"That's what Miss Ina said." I sigh, running my fingers through my hair.

"I still can't believe that you stayed the night with her—and that she didn't suffocate you in your sleep."

"She's actually really nice," I admit. Libby's eyes go wide, making me smile. "I think I actually might like her." I laugh and she snorts, which makes me laugh harder.

"What are you two laughing about?"

Hearing my dad's voice, I jump out of my chair and rush across the room into his arms. They wrap around me tightly. I close my eyes, soaking in the feeling for a moment. Even though it's only been a few days since I saw him, I've missed my dad and his ability to make everything better.

"Hey, kid." His arms tighten when mine do, and I feel his lips on the top of my head.

"Hey, Dad." I tip my head back and smile up at him.

"You okay?" His thumb touches the skin under my eye, and I know he can see the dark circles there, brought on by crying most of the night and waking up way too early this morning.

"I'm okay. Better now that I know Levi will be okay," I say.

His eyes close briefly. As a cop himself, our dad expressed his concerns when Fawn and Levi first started dating. He reminded not only Fawn but also all of us that being the spouse of a police officer is not an easy job. There's a risk anytime an officer puts on the badge and leaves the house. But we all told him that there's a risk anytime *anyone* leaves the house—especially nowadays. The world is a scary place.

"Where's Mom?" Libby asks, shoving me out of the way like she's been doing since the day she was born. She hugs Dad.

"Hey, sweetheart," he laughs while kissing the top of her head. "Your mom's with Levi's mom. They just left to run over to Fawn's place and get her some clothes. Your sister's refused to leave Levi's side."

"Libby and I could have gone to get her some stuff," I say.

He smiles at me, reaching out to touch my cheek.

"It's good they went. They needed to feel like they were doing something useful. Besides, they've been driving Levi and Fawn crazy with their puttering around, trying to fluff his pillows and bickering with the nurses about giving him more pain meds when he's told them he doesn't need them."

I laugh. My mom *would* do that. She doesn't understand the meaning of boundaries. Levi's mom seems to be cut from the same cloth.

"Are you and Mom going to stay in the city?" Libby asks before shoving a handful of M&M's into her mouth.

"We're staying at Fawn's place. Levi's parents are going to stay at his place." He looks between the two of us, and his face softens. "You girls should head home. They'll be kicking everyone out before long, anyway. You two can come back in the morning."

"We'll just say bye to Fawn and Levi first," Libby says.

I grab my purse and follow her and my dad down the hall. As soon as we enter Levi's room, I smile at him.

He presses a finger to his lips, gesturing for us to be quiet since Fawn is asleep on the bed, tucked into his side.

"We just wanted to say we're heading out. Tell Fawn to call us in the morning."

I lean down and kiss his cheek, but he grabs my hand before I can lean back.

"Please go check on Wesley," he says.

I pull back to look at him and swallow when I see the worry in his eyes.

"I will," I agree.

He lets me go. I watch Libby give him a hug, and then I walk over to my dad and wrap my arms around his waist. I rest my head on his shoulder.

"You okay, kid?"

"Yeah," I lie, giving him a squeeze before letting him go so he can hug Libby. "We'll see you tomorrow."

"See you tomorrow." He kisses Libby's forehead and opens the door for us.

Once we're in the hall, I pull out my cell phone and try to call Wesley. He doesn't answer. Swallowing over the realization that I may have completely ruined things between us, I pull in a breath and look at Libby.

"I'm going to stop by Wesley's. Will you be okay getting a cab on your own?"

"Of course." She reaches over to take my hand, then softens her voice. "Things will be okay."

"I hope so," I agree.

She squeezes my fingers, then lets them go as we head through the automatic doors and step outside. We spy a few cabs parked on the curb and both head in that direction.

"Call if you're not going to be home, so I don't worry."

"Sure, Mom." I roll my eyes.

She laughs while getting into the cab parked behind mine.

When I arrive at Wesley's place about twenty minutes later, I feel my stomach in my throat. I head down to his apartment door, knock and ring the bell, and wait for him to answer.

Time ticks by. No answer. This lets me know that either he's really not home or he knows it's me and doesn't want to see me. After ten minutes, I give up and wave down a cab. As soon as I'm in the backseat, the driver asks me where I'm going. Without thinking, I give him the name of the bar where Wesley and I met. I know it's a long shot, but it's the only place I can think he might be.

"Please be here," I whisper to myself as I open the door to Charlie's and step inside.

I scan the crowded room and let out a relieved breath when I spot Wesley sitting at the bar—alone. His shoulders are slumped like he's carrying the weight of the world on them.

"Do you need some company?" I ask, sliding onto the empty stool next to his.

His head slowly turns my direction.

"What are you doing here?" he asks.

I hate the hurt I see staring back at me. I hate knowing that I'm part of the reason that he's hurting even more.

"It's kind of a sad story." I wave off the bartender when she comes over to ask if I want a drink. I place my purse on the top of the bar. "You see, I messed up with this guy I like. I've stupidly been trying to push him away. I thought that if I could end it before he did that I would be saving myself from embarrassment. I thought it was only a matter of time until he figured out that I wasn't who he wanted."

"Did he let you push him away?" he asks, holding my gaze.

I duck my head.

"I don't know yet. But if he does, I deserve it," I whisper the truth, feeling tears burn my throat.

"He'd be an idiot to let you go," he says softly. He touches his fingers to my chin to lift my eyes up to his.

Hope fills my chest.

"I'm not sure about that. I'm kind of a pain in the ass, and I have a tendency to run when things scare me," I say.

He grunts and turns toward me on the stool so that his knees lock around mine.

"Are you done running?" he asks while sliding his hands up my thighs, making my breath catch.

"I'm scared," I admit.

He closes his eyes and touches his forehead to mine.

"Me too." His admission catches me off guard, and my body jolts. "But I'm not running, and I need to know that you're going to give us a chance—a real chance," he murmurs, sliding his hands around my waist as I wind my arms around his neck to get closer.

"I can do that," I agree.

He stands, forcing me to stand with him. His hands move to my ass, and he lifts me off the ground.

"What are you doing?" I ask.

"Taking you out of here." He dips his mouth close to my ear and says, "I need to be alone with you. I need to be inside of you."

"Oh . . . ," I whisper.

"Now wrap your legs around my waist and grab your purse," he commands.

I do as he says, having no doubt that everyone in the bar is watching us.

"So bossy." I roll my eyes, and he smiles, touching his lips to mine. "Are you still mad at me?" I ask as he carries me out of the bar and onto the sidewalk.

He sticks out one hand for a cab while keeping me propped up against his body with the other one still under my bottom.

"I wasn't mad. I was disappointed."

"I think that's worse," I admit.

His mouth touches mine once more, but then he makes it even better by sliding his tongue between my lips.

Nipping at my lip, he pulls back. "No more hiding, no more running."

"No more running," I say as he helps me into the backseat of a cab that stops. "Are you sure you are ready for my mom to know about us? As you may have figured out when you met her at Thanksgiving, she is insane. Nosy and insane."

"You said insane twice."

"Trust me, it *should* be repeated more than once. I don't think you understand. She tried to set me up with her fifty-year-old neighbor because she is desperate for grandbabies," I say, watching his eyes narrow. Rolling my eyes at his reaction, I smack his chest. "I didn't even talk to him. I couldn't get you off my mind no matter how hard I tried."

"Good."

"You *would* think it's good that you've taken over my brain," I say quietly as he lifts my hand and kisses my wrist.

"It's only fair—you seem to have taken over mine," he says.

My stomach flutters.

My mind screams, *Please don't be too good to be true!*

Chapter 6

Reckless

Wesley

"Do you have something I can wear to bed?"

At Mackenzie's question, I set my gun on the top of the table and lift my head. I see her standing across from me, looking more beautiful than ever. It's not that she's wearing makeup or that the button-up silk top she has on outlines her breasts and accentuates her waist or that the heels she has on make her legs look miles long. It's that for the first time since meeting her, I can see that she's really *here* with me. She's not trying to plan an escape or trying to come up with an excuse for why this won't work between us.

"No," I answer as I remove my holster.

"No?" She frowns. "You don't have a T-shirt I can borrow?"

"Nope." I hide my smile when she plants her hands on her hips.

"Why not?"

"Why would I give you a shirt when I'm just going to take it off as soon as we get into bed?" I ask, raising a brow.

Her gaze turns heated. "You seem pretty sure of yourself."

"You gonna deny me?" I ask, watching the pulse in her neck start to thump away. "You won't deny me." I answer the question for her. "I know you want my mouth and my cock. I can see your nipples through that shirt, so I know they're hard. Just like I know that in a few minutes, when I run my fingers between your folds, you'll already be wet for me. And I know because you keep squeezing your thighs together, trying to get rid of that ache you know only I can fix." I take a step toward her, watching as she squeezes her legs together once more. "One of the things we've got figured out is chemistry, gorgeous. We have that in the bag. I can't be in the same room with you without getting hard," I say as I take her hand and place it over the front of my pants. My cock is testing the limits of my zipper. "I've never wanted anyone the way I want you, and I know by the way that your body reacts to me and my touch that you feel the same."

"You've never felt like this about *anyone* else?" she asks, softly searching my gaze for a lie.

"Never," I admit as I start to unbutton her top. It's true. I haven't felt like this about another woman. I have never wanted another woman the way I want her. I take a seat on one of the chairs in the kitchen and pull her to me so she's standing between my spread legs. "You make me crazy." I kiss between her breasts.

"Just crazy?" she asks.

I pause from working at her buttons and look up at her gorgeous face.

"You make me want more." I continue undoing the buttons and kissing down her chest and stomach until her shirt falls completely open. I roam my hands up her waist, over her breasts, and onto her shoulders.

"More?" Her breath hitches as I slide the shirt off. I reach around to unhook her bra, letting it fall to the floor.

"More." I skim my thumbs over her nipples before cupping her breasts. "A future."

"Oh . . ." Her breath hitches again as I lean forward and take one nipple into my mouth. I lick its tip before blowing across it and watching it tighten.

"Do you still want a shirt?" I pull my mouth away to look up at her.

Her head shakes side to side, and I smile. I take her other nipple into my mouth while pulling her down to straddle my lap.

"Wesley." She holds on to my shoulders as I suck and lick her nipple while tugging the neglected one between my fingers.

"Lock your hands behind your back, gorgeous." I reach over and grab my cuffs off the table. She pants and leans back. I don't know what she sees in my gaze, but her eyes close, and she takes her hands off my shoulders and does as I say. "Good girl." I cuff her wrists together, then pull them down until her body arches back. "I like you like this. At my mercy, unable to run. I think I may have to keep you like this all the time." I lick over one nipple again, then the other. I listen to her moan, feel her hips shift until her core is directly over my cock. I'm so hard, it's painful.

"Wesley, please . . ."

"Please what?" I slide my hands up her waist and then back down. I run my fingers along the top of her pants. "What do you want?"

"You. I need you."

"Are you wet?"

"Yes."

The word hisses out as I flick open the button of her slacks and slide down her zipper.

Seeing the barely-there panties covering her pussy, I growl. "Up." Once she's standing in front of me, I help her out of them. Before guiding her back onto my lap, I adjust her so her back is arched and her pussy is exposed. "Are you okay like this?"

"Yes." She nods, swallowing. My cock throbs. I kiss along her jaw, down her neck, and then over her breasts. Her breath hitches as I slide two fingers down between her folds and on either side of her clit. I slide them deep inside of her. "Ride my fingers."

"Wesley . . . ?" I hear the apprehension in her voice.

"Ride them. I want to watch you make yourself come." I roll her clit with my thumb, and pink spreads from her cheeks and down her neck. "Don't be shy, gorgeous. I plan on getting to know your body better than you know it yourself. I plan on knowing every single inch of you, inside and out," I say against her mouth before taking a kiss. I lean back to watch her ride my fingers to orgasm. Freeing myself from my jeans, I wrap my hand around the base of my cock and watch her lick her lips. "Do you want this?"

"Yes." Rubbing the head over her clit, I groan when she arches back. I slide the tip inside. "You're soaked." I lock my hands around her hips to hold her in place. "What are you doing, gorgeous?"

"I don't know," she whispers, rocking against me—and proving that she knows *exactly* what she's doing.

"Mackenzie," I warn as she swivels her hips. Already strung tight, I know I'm two seconds from losing it when her hair slides across my skin. "Do not fucking tease me."

"I'm not . . . ," she lies on a moan.

My muscles tighten even farther in response. Sliding one hand up her thigh, I roll her clit with my thumb and cup a breast with my free hand, tugging at her nipple.

"Wesley."

"I told you not to tease . . . dammit!" I hiss. My neck arches as she glides slowly down my length. I know I should tell her that we should be using a condom, but hearing the sounds she's making and feeling her walls tighten around me makes it impossible to stop. "If you're going to start this, you better be a good girl and ride me hard and fast," I growl.

She moans again, lifting and falling on top of me exactly like I instructed. Sliding my hand up to the back of her neck, I drag her mouth down to me. I keep her locked in place so that I can kiss her and thrust my tongue into her mouth, mimicking the way she's fucking me.

"Wesley, I'm so close," she pants.

I know she is—her walls are squeezing me so tight that it's almost painful.

"Fuck me, Mackenzie. Don't stop until I say," I tell her.

She sits back on my lap, taking me hard—so hard that my spine starts to tingle and my balls draw up.

Knowing I'm about to lose it, I warn her, "I'm not wearing a condom. You keep fucking me, and I'm going to come inside your hot, tight, pussy bare."

"Come inside me," she whimpers.

I let out a curse, wrap my hands around her hips, and pull her down onto my hard length over and over until we both shout out our uninhibited release.

Breathing heavily, I tuck my face into her neck and wrap my arms around her to keep her right where she is. Right where she belongs.

"Twice," I murmur.

Her body jolts before relaxing.

"I know."

"You need to get on birth control," I tell her, unlocking the cuffs from her wrist and letting them fall to the floor. I gather her in my arms.

"I know," she agrees again.

My hold tightens as an image of her holding a little girl with red hair fills my mind.

"I'll make an appointment."

"All right." I roam my hand down her back, then back up and into her hair. "Do you feel like showering with me, or do you want to sleep?"

"I'll shower," she says, sounding half-asleep. I smile as she whispers, "But you're going to have to carry me. I don't know if my legs are up to holding my weight yet."

"I can do that." I stand on shaking legs while staying inside her. She tightens her legs around my waist and her arms around my neck.

"Is that supposed to be possible?" she whimpers, digging her nails into my shoulders.

I start to get hard again.

"With you, yeah," I say, walking into the bathroom and flipping on the light before reaching in to start up the shower. Once the steam begins to fill the room, I step over the ledge and into the tub. I listen to her gasp as my cock slides even farther inside. "One more time. Tomorrow we'll stop being reckless."

"Tomorrow," she agrees as I press her back into the tile and take her again under the warm water.

~

Feeling the bed shift, I jerk awake. I grab hold of Mackenzie and pull her back down into the bed with me. "Where are you going?"

"I just need to use the restroom."

Her quiet words fill me with relief. I loosen my hold, then feel her lips touch my shoulder before she exits the bed. Looking for my cell phone on my nightstand, I find it and pick it up to check the time. It's already seven, which means I need to get up for work soon. Hearing the toilet flush and the water turn on, I wait for her to come back to bed. I smile as I watch her run naked across the room and dive under the covers.

"It's like the Arctic in here. Do you have the heat on?" She shivers, and I grin as she tucks herself tightly against me, trying to absorb my heat.

"I like sleeping in the cold. I like it more that you have no choice but to use me for body heat," I say.

She hits my chest playfully, making me laugh.

Kissing the top of her head, I ask, "What are your plans for today?"

"I'll probably go with Libby to check on Fawn and Levi, then see if my parents need anything. They're going to be here for a few days," she says as her fingers draw a random pattern over my heart. "What about you?"

"I have work, but I'd like to see you after."

"I'd like that."

Rolling her to her back, I hover over her and slide my fingers through her hair. "Pack an overnight bag. I'll pick you up tonight when I get off work."

"This is more than just sex, right?"

Her question catches me off guard. I freeze for a moment, then reach over her head and turn on the bedside lamp. Looking down at her once my eyes have adjusted to the bright light, I take her face between my palms.

"This is way more than just sex. I know I can't keep my hands off you when you're close, but I also can't keep my mind off you when you're gone. Don't tell me that you've really been thinking that this was just about hooking up?"

"I haven't." She shakes her head and closes her eyes for a moment before looking at me once more. "I've never had a one-night stand before. I—"

Covering her lips with a finger, I shake my head.

"You still *haven't* had a one-night stand. We didn't just hook up and call it quits. Even if you hadn't forgotten your phone, I would have eventually found you."

"You would have?"

"Don't you feel this thing between us? How strong it is? Do you think that I could just let you go without trying to find out what exactly it is?" I kiss her jaw. "Since the second I saw you, I knew that I wanted you. But from the moment you smiled at me and told me that you got stood up, I knew that there was something about you that I had to have. Lucky for me your date didn't show up that night. If he had, I can't guarantee that I wouldn't have tried to talk to you anyway, even with him sitting right next to you."

"Oh," she whispers as a small smile plays on her lips.

"I know that nothing about us is traditional, but I'm okay with that as long as there *is* an us. So are we on the same page now?"

"I think so."

"Good." I kiss her, then roll to my back and pull her over on top of me.

"Wesley . . ."

"Yeah?" I run my hand down her arm as she slides up my body so she can rest her chin on my chest. I slide her hand up the side of my neck before wrapping it around my jaw.

"I know you may not want to, but if you *do* want to talk about what happened last night, or"—she pauses—"what happened before, I'm here," she says quietly.

My stomach muscles tighten, and my heart constricts.

"Thanks, gorgeous," I say quietly.

She turns her head and kisses my chest before resting her cheek against my pec. In a few moments, she's back asleep.

～

Before my boot even makes it over the threshold at the hospital, I hear my name. I look up to find Mackenzie's mom rushing toward me down the empty hall. She's wearing dark slacks and a Christmas sweater with bells on it. I had called Mackenzie a little while before, and she told me that she and Libby were at the hospital. I figured I could kill two birds with one stone: get a few minutes with my girl and check on my partner.

Now, seeing the look on Katie's face, I remember that Mackenzie also mentioned telling her parents about us. I should have held off trying to see her until this evening. Mackenzie was right—her mom is crazy.

"Oh, I'm so happy to see you! So, so happy." She pats the side of my face before yanking my head down. Forced to bend, I hug her

84

awkwardly as she kisses my cheek. "I knew, I just *knew* that you and our Mac would hit it off. I have a sick sense about these things."

"I think you mean *sixth* sense, Mom," Libby says, catching up to her and giving me a one-armed hug while rolling her eyes.

"That's what I said—a sixth sense." Katie shoos away her youngest with one hand and takes mine with the other. "Mac is in talking to Fawn and Levi. I'll lead you that way, and we can talk."

"Mom, what did Mac say about scaring off her boyfriend?"

"I'm not scaring him off," she says as she turns to look up at me. "Right?"

"Not at all," I deny.

She smiles, wiggling her head side to side in a way that reminds me of a hyper Chihuahua I had growing up.

"So . . . before we get into the room, I want to talk to you about Christmas. I know you mentioned at Thanksgiving that your family lives in Seattle, and that you would be here in New York for the holiday, so I wanted to invite you myself to Long Island."

"That's really nice, but my mom and stepdad will be coming here," I say.

She stops to look at me.

"Oh! Well, I'd love to meet your mother! Bring her along." She smiles, and I fight back a laugh.

Maybe Mackenzie had the right idea about keeping our relationship from her family. I can see now that her mom is going to be difficult to disappoint—and even harder to keep out of our business.

"I'll see how my mom feels about that. I'm sure that she would like to meet you, too."

"Meet who?"

Lifting my head, I smile at Mackenzie. She's standing just outside Levi's door wearing jeans and a sweatshirt that is about ten sizes too big for her small frame. Her hair is down in a wavy mess. It reminds me of what she looks like after we make love.

"Hey, gorgeous," I say.

Her eyes soften for a brief moment as she looks at me. Then she looks at her mom and narrows them.

"Who are you meeting?"

"Wesley's mom, when she comes into town for Christmas," Katie says.

The color drains from Mackenzie's face as her eyes fly to meet mine. "Your mom is coming into town?" she asks.

Libby takes Katie's hand and begins to drag her into the room. She closes the door behind them, leaving Mackenzie in the hall with me.

"She is." I cross my arms over my chest. "Why do you have the look on your face that you always get when you're about to run away?"

"I don't."

"You do—I have that look memorized," I say.

She looks away, takes a deep breath, and then looks at me once more.

"Do you want me to meet her?" she asks.

I know she's nervous by the way she wrings her hands together.

"Yeah, I'd like you to meet her. I know she's going to want to meet you, too."

"But I'm a tomboy!" she blurts with wide eyes. I frown, confused. "Pardon?"

"I'm a tomboy. How will your mom feel about you dating a tomboy?"

"Who the hell told you that you're a tomboy?"

"I've always been a tomboy. I like wearing jeans and sneakers. I don't like makeup. I love sports, beer, and hanging out with the guys."

"I already know all this about you. I know that you're a woman who likes to be comfortable, who looks amazing without makeup, who enjoys sports and beer and has male friends. Who the fuck cares about any of that? You're beautiful, and my mom will think so, too."

"But I'm not like most women."

"Thank fuck for that, gorgeous. If you *were* like most women, I wouldn't want you like I do." I uncross my arms and step toward her. "Now stop stressing about this. If you can handle *your* mom, I guarantee you can handle mine. She'll adore you."

"If you say so," she huffs as I drag her against me and plant a kiss on her lips.

"I know so." I kiss her again as she winds her arms around my neck.

"Is it weird that I missed you today?" The question is barely audible, but I hear it. Relief fills me—she's feeling exactly what I am.

"Probably, but I don't give a fuck about that, either." I kiss her again and she smiles.

"I kinda like you, Wesley Jameson."

"I just straight-up like you, Mackenzie Reed," I say.

She smiles, dancing her fingers across my neck. Her eyes watch them move across my skin.

"Why don't you call me Mac, like everyone else?"

"Because I don't want to be like everyone else to you," I say.

She looks up at me, and her lips part.

"Are you two going to stand out there all day, or are you going to come in?" Levi breaks into the moment.

Mackenzie blinks, then shakes her head before looking at him.

"Glad to see you up and about, man." I shake his hand and he gives me a one-arm hug.

"Thanks, man."

"How are you feeling?" I ask when he steps back and runs his good hand through his hair.

"All right. Ready to get out of this place. I don't know how much more I can take."

"Oh, stop being an angry bear," Fawn says as she comes toward us down the hall.

I see how he turns to look at her, his gaze turning soft.

"I'm not angry."

87

"You've been growling at everyone since we woke up," she tells him, tucking herself into his good side and resting her hand on his stomach.

"I woke up with both of our moms hovering over us. That's not exactly my favorite way to start the day," he huffs.

Mackenzie and Fawn laugh.

"I know, but they are just trying to help. What are you doing up anyway? You are supposed to be in bed."

"I needed to get out of the room for a minute. Plus, you were gone a long time. I thought that you were just going to the gift shop," he tells her.

She shakes her head.

"I was gone ten minutes tops. Now come on. It's time to go back to bed. The doctor said to take it easy."

She ushers him back around and through the door toward the bed. The moms are in there at a small table, playing cards with Libby.

After saying a quick hello to everyone, I head to the bed. Fawn is helping Levi get back in.

"I can't stay long. Someone needs to do a shit ton of paperwork, and since my partner decided he'd take a paid vacation, I got stuck with it," I joke.

Levi grins. "Thanks for that, man."

"No problem." I pat his good shoulder lightly. "If you need anything, just send a text."

"I might need you to help me escape," he says quietly.

Fawn narrows her eyes at him, and he shrugs while giving her a smile.

"Like I said, just send a text." I look at Mackenzie. "Walk me out?"

"Sure."

When we reach my truck, I make out with her for ten minutes before I head back to the station.

Feeling Mackenzie's warm breath brush across my neck, I tighten my fingers around her hip with one hand and sift my fingers through her soft hair with the other. She fell asleep twenty minutes ago, sprawled out on top of me on the couch wearing one of my T-shirts and a pair of my boxers. We had just eaten half a pizza and watched *Die Hard* and *Die Hard 2*.

When I had asked her what she wanted to watch, she told me she loves action movies. I honestly expected her to tell me that she loved romantic comedies or dramas—the types of movies that make me fall asleep halfway through. Once again, she surprised me.

Just like she surprised me on our first date by not wanting to eat at the restaurant I had chosen for us. Most women I've dated would rather pick at a forty-dollar salad than eat a twenty-dollar pizza covered in meat and cheese. Then again, I'm learning quickly that she isn't like most women I've known—she's better. She's exactly what I didn't know I was looking for. I love that she has no problem devouring a pizza without apology and looking sexy doing it, and that in bed she gives as good as she gets. I like that she's comfortable in her own skin. That she doesn't feel a need to hide herself under makeup. I appreciate that she's strong and independent, but that she can be vulnerable at times.

I know without a doubt she was made just for me. Now I just need to convince her that I was made for her, too.

Chapter 7

Girl Code

Mac

Lifting my head and seeing Edward walk through my office door, I smile and push my chair away from my desk. "Hey, you." I stand and walk around my desk to greet him with a hug. "What are you doing here?" I let him go and take a step back.

"I came to check on you. I haven't seen you in a while. What's been going on?"

"Work. You know how it is." I shrug and take a seat on the edge of my desk while he sits in one of the chairs across from me.

"Just work?" he asks curiously.

"Well . . . when I'm not working, I'm spending time with Wesley," I say.

He tips his head to the side. "Is Wesley the big guy I saw the last time I was here?" He raises his arms away from his body like he has too many muscles.

"Yeah." I smile.

He rubs his hand down his jaw. "He seemed a little intense," he says.

My stomach tingles as I remember the way his intensity feels whenever it's directed at me.

"He's a cop." I use that as explanation, and he nods. "So did you just come by to check on me?"

"Actually, I wanted to see if you had time to give me a massage. Bonnie and I are heading to her parents' for Christmas, and I've been stressed."

"Why? I thought you got along with her family."

"I do get along with them, but . . ." He pulls a box out of his pocket and flips the top open. "Carrying this thing around is making me anxious."

"You're asking Bonnie to marry you!"

"That's the plan." He snaps the box closed and shoves it back in his pocket.

"I'm happy for you. The ring is beautiful. She's going to freak when she sees it." I stand and give him another hug. "I wish I had time to help you out today, but I have clients back-to-back. Everyone wants to come in before they go away for Christmas. You should have called me," I tell him as the buzzer next to my door goes off, letting me know that my next client has already arrived.

"I should have." He moves his neck side to side, cracking it, then pulls out his phone as it rings. "One second." He looks at the screen before he puts it to his ear to answer. "Hey, baby."

Thinking that it's Bonnie, I smile at him.

"Yeah, I'll meet you there. But remember—you can't call me next week since I'll be with Bonnie at her parents' house," he says.

That smile slides right off my face, and nausea turns my stomach. I fight the urge to kick him in his balls or pick up my stapler and toss it at his stupid, fat, cheating head.

"All right. I'm just gonna say bye to my friend, then I'll be over that way. Yeah, see you soon." He ends the call and puts the phone in the inside pocket of his jacket just as my next client, Dorothy, comes into my office.

Giving her a smile, I look back at Edward.

He leans down to kiss my cheek. "We'll talk after the holiday."

"Sure." Swallowing down bile, I watch him go. I wonder how the hell I didn't see it before, how the hell I didn't notice that he is a complete man whore and a huge dick.

Pushing thoughts of him away, I lead Dorothy down the hall and into the massage room. I instruct her to get undressed and onto the table, then tell her that I'll be back in a few minutes.

After I leave, I rush to my desk and pick up my cell. I group text Libby and Fawn.

Edward just stopped by my office. He showed me the ring he is going to use to propose to his girlfriend, then he went to go meet a woman that I'm pretty sure he is cheating on Bonnie with.

Fawn: Shut up.

Libby: Oh my god you so dodged a bullet.

Fawn: His poor girlfriend.

Me: I know, I feel like I should warn her.

Libby: Don't do it. She will find out on her own. He won't be able to hide it forever.

Fawn: I would want to know if Levi was cheating on me. I think you should tell her. It's girl code.

Me: I'll have to think about it.

Libby: I swear you two never listen to me. Whatever . . . I have to work. We will talk over Christmas shopping.

Me: <3

Fawn: Talk soon.

Setting my cell phone down on the top of my desk, I get back to work. That is, I *try* to. For the most part, I spend the day trying to think of a way to tell Bonnie that Edward is cheating on her without telling her directly.

~

Taking a sip of my soda, I stare at Wesley over the rim of the cup. He stares back at me with a disbelieving look in his eyes. I've just told him about Edward's phone call in my office earlier today and my plan to send Bonnie an unmarked letter with a note explaining that she should not marry Edward because he is a cheating dick.

"No." He shakes his head. "You need to stay out of it."

"I can't just stay out of it—it goes against girl code. If you were cheating on me, I would want to know about it," I say as he finishes chopping up an onion to add to a pan on the stove that already contains ground beef and chopped tomatoes.

It's weird to have someone cook for me, but he's done it every night without question since we really got together. His only request is that I sit with him while he prepares it.

"First of all, I would *never* cheat on you. Cheating is something cowards do. Second, I don't give a fuck about girl code. You don't need to be the one who tells her about her boyfriend being a piece of shit."

"Who else is going to tell her, then?" I ask, throwing my hand in the air.

He moves toward me, takes my cup from my hand, and sets it on the counter next to me before pushing my legs apart to stand between them.

"Gorgeous, I get that you feel she needs to know, but I don't like the idea of *you* being the one to tell her about it. She could freak—or he could."

"It's going to be anonymous . . . ," I remind him.

He sighs.

"I won't leave any trace that it was me who told her. I won't say a name or anything. I will just say something like 'your man is a cheating dick.'"

I expect that to make him smile, but it doesn't.

He moves his face closer to mine and wraps a hand around my jaw. "Please, just leave it alone."

Searching his gaze and seeing worry there, I chew on the inside of my cheek. I want to ask him why, but I don't want him to shut down on me. Not when we've had a great couple of weeks. Letting out a huff, I give in.

"Fine. I'll leave it alone."

"Thank you."

"Whatever." I pout, and he smiles, then kisses it away.

"Are you excited about tomorrow?" he asks.

My stomach instantly fills with nervous butterflies. His mom and stepdad are flying in. Christmas is in three days, and since I only have one client in the morning, I stupidly agreed to go with him to the airport to pick them up.

"So totally excited!" I lie.

"Liar." He kisses my forehead. "It will be fine. My mom will love you."

"If you say so." I kiss his scruffy jaw, then smile when my stomach growls. "Are you going to keep kissing me, or are you going to cook me dinner?"

"I don't know. I like kissing you."

"Me too." I kiss him again and again.

About ten minutes later, when my stomach growls loudly, he finally pulls away.

"So what are you making anyway?" I ask him as he grabs a pepper and starts to chop it up.

"Tacos."

"Yum." My mouth waters, and he smiles at me. "Did your mom teach you how to cook?" I ask, picking my drink back up.

"She did. After the summer of hot dogs, she taught me. She figured that I would need to know how to cook for myself so I could do it while I was at my dad's house. The first thing she taught me how to make was fajitas. The second was lasagna."

"My mom never taught us how to cook. I think she secretly liked keeping us dependent on her for food."

"I'll teach you." He smiles at me, and my heart does some weird double beat.

"You will?"

"Of course. I'm not the best cook, but I know the basics. I can show you those."

"Well, I know nothing, so you are already a million times better than me." I laugh and take another sip of soda. I love this. I love how easy things are between us. Spending time with him is like hanging out with my best friend. That's something I've never had with anyone before him.

"What are you thinking about?" he asks as he pulls a pack of tortillas out of the fridge.

"How easy this whole relationship business is with you," I admit.

I watch as his face gets soft and his eyes get warm.

"Have I told you today how much I like you?" he asks.

My heart skips and my stomach tingles.

"Not *today*."

"I like you a lot."

"Good. Because I like you a lot, too."

I reach forward, grab hold of his sweater, and pull him toward me. Kissing him once, I let him go and then hop down off the counter to help him finish up dinner.

We eat while watching TV. Then we head to bed for the night, where we do a lot more than just sleep.

~

"Calm down."

"You calm down!" I snap at Wesley as his hand tightens around mine. I wonder if he's afraid I'm going to run away like a coward. I might. "I think this is too soon. Don't you think it's too soon for me to meet your mom? Isn't that something couples do after they have been seeing each other for months and months? Sometimes years and ye—"

His mouth crashes down on mine, and his tongue slips between my parted and stunned lips. Cupping my cheeks, he tips my head to the side to deepen the kiss. It makes me forget that we're in the middle of a crowed airport where hundreds of people can see us.

"It's not too soon," he growls, pulling his mouth away from mine.

"Okay," I breathe as my eyes flutter open. "I'm just a little bit scared."

"I know you are. I knew you were this morning, because you asked me a million times what you should wear, if you should wear makeup, and how you should do your hair."

"It wasn't a million times," I mumble.

He grins. "Okay, a hundred thousand times."

"Whatever." I blow a strand of hair out of my face.

He runs his thumbs across my cheeks.

"Worst-case scenario, my mom hates you. So I never talk to her again."

"Your mom wouldn't be very happy with that plan, sugar pants," a woman says from behind me.

I close my eyes and groan internally, realizing the woman is his mom.

I force myself to open my eyes, then turn with Wesley to face his mom and her husband. I don't know what I was expecting his mom to look like, but the blonde standing across from me who looks a lot like Michelle Pfeiffer wasn't it.

Letting me go, Wesley greets them with a joint hug before stepping back and placing his arm around my waist.

"Mom, I'd like you to meet Mackenzie. Mackenzie, my mom, Monica."

She smiles at him before looking at me.

"It's so nice to meet you." I stick out my hand.

Her eyes drop to my outstretched hand, and she rolls them before pulling me in for a tight hug, saying close to my ear, "We don't shake hands."

"It's nice to finally meet you," I whisper as her arms tighten around me.

"You too," she whispers back, letting me go and taking her husband's hand. "Mac?" She pauses, tipping her head to the side, studying me briefly. "Can I call you Mac?"

"Of course. Everyone does—except Wesley," I say.

His arm wraps around my shoulder, and his lips touch the top of my head.

"Mac, this is my husband, Peter."

"Nice to meet you, Peter." I smile and try to give him a handshake, but once more I'm pulled in for an unexpected hug.

"Nice to meet you, Mac."

"You too," I agree as he lets me go.

"How many bags did you bring, Mom?" Wesley asks as he tucks me right back under his arm.

"Just two," she says.

Peter clears his throat.

She glares at him. "Fine, three. But one of them doesn't even count—all it has in it is my makeup and meds."

"What about my bag? You took up all its space by shoving your shoes in there."

"You can't complain about that now. You should have complained when we were home and I was doing it. Now it's too late."

"I'm not complaining, doll, just pointing out that you have a lot more stuff than you say you do."

"Well, I had to bring gifts for my son and his girlfriend."

My eyes widen. I haven't gotten her anything for Christmas. Thank goodness I still have a shopping trip planned with Libby and Fawn for tomorrow. It's something we've done every year since we were old enough to go out on our own.

"Let's go see if your bags have come out. While we wait, you can tell us about your flight," Wesley suggests, leading us all toward baggage claim.

He keeps a tight hold on my hand—he's probably more afraid now than ever that I'm going to take off on him. To be honest, for once I'm not thinking about it. All I can think about is the fact that Wesley has made it a point to remind me over and over that I mean something to him and that he has chosen me and will keep on choosing me.

"Are you doing okay?" he asks against my ear.

I tip my head back to look at him and smile. "Totally okay." I squeeze his fingers, then lean back against him.

I listen as his mom tells us about their trip, and I do it smiling, too.

Chapter 8

THE GIFT THAT KEEPS ON GIVING

MAC

I knock on Miss Ina's door. I wait for her to answer for a minute, then knock again and press my ear to the door to see if I can hear her coming. I haven't seen her in a few days, and I'm honestly a little worried. "Miss Ina?" I knock again.

"Child, if you don't stop knocking on my door and give me a few minutes to walk across the room to answer it, I'm going to beat you with my walker when I open it up," she grouches.

I let out a relieved breath and smile.

"Hurry up!" I shout.

I hear her huff on the other side, which makes my smile even bigger.

"Why did I have to come along for this?" Libby asks.

She's next to me, standing with her arms crossed over her chest.

"Because I thought it would be nice if you were here when we invite her over to Christmas dinner. She's alone."

"She really did put a spell on you, didn't she?"

"I told you. I like her." I shrug, then knock again just to annoy Ina.

"What's so important that you need to wake me from my afternoon nap?" Miss Ina answers as she finally opens the door.

I grin, then give her a hug that she tries to pull away from. I don't let her get far.

"You're coming with us on Christmas."

"No, I'm not." She shakes her head and attempts to shut the door, but I block it with my foot before she can.

"Yes, you are. I even ordered us a car service for the morning of so we don't have to take the train out to Long Island."

"Child, I'm staying home on Christmas. Now go on." She tries to shoo us away.

Before, that might have worked, but now I know that she's a big softie. I'm not going anywhere.

"Miss Ina, I'm sorry to be the one to tell you this, but the day you made me tea and let me cry on your shoulder and then sleep on your couch is the day you and I became friends. I don't let my friends sit alone at home on Christmas, so Christmas morning you will be coming with me and Libby to our parents' house—even if I have to break into your apartment and drag you with me."

I smile, and she glares at me. Then she glares at Libby.

"I should call the law on you two for harassing me."

"Do it." I raise a brow, and she huffs again.

Libby tenses at my side, not knowing that the woman is all bark and no bite.

"Fine," Miss Ina says, finally giving in. "I'll come—but only because I want to." She shakes her head as she starts to shut the door again, but I move my foot back in to block it again.

"Promise me." I hold out my pinkie toward her.

"I should have left you to cry in the hall," she says.

I don't move anything more than one eyebrow, which I raise.

"Fine. I promise." She slaps my hand, then slams the door.

"She's still scary," Libby says, taking my arm and pulling me along with her.

"I heard that! I'm glad you think so, seeing how your sister's forgotten!" Miss Ina shouts through the door.

I laugh along with Libby as we head up the stairs to our apartment.

After entering, I kick off my shoes and sigh. "It feels like I haven't been here in forever," I say as we plop down on the couch next to each other. I haven't been home for weeks. I've been spending all my time with Wesley, but with his mom and stepdad sleeping in his bed while he's on the couch, I won't be staying with him again until after Christmas.

"You haven't, and it's a lot quieter without you around," Libby says.

I look at her and instantly feel guilty for not having been home much.

"I'm sorry."

"Don't be. Honestly, it's been nice." She smirks. "Do you think that you and Wesley are going to move in together sometime soon?" she asks, sounding way too hopeful. I pick up one of the pillows and hit her with it, making her laugh. "Seriously, though. What are you guys planning on doing?"

"I don't know. It will probably be a while before we take that step. Our relationship has been moving too quickly from the beginning, and I think that we need some time to get to know each other before we make any big commitments."

"That's probably smart, but then again, you *have* been with him every day and every night. It doesn't make sense to live here, paying rent, while spending all your time there with him."

"True." I hug the pillow to my chest. "But if I was to move out, do you think you could afford this place on your own?"

"Yes, Mom." She rolls her eyes. "Plus, I've been tucking away the extra money I've been making at Tony's the last couple weeks."

"How's it been, working there?"

Ever since the day I told Libby about Tony being in the hospital and Antonio needing help at the pizza parlor, she's been going in a few days a week to help out with waiting tables and answering the phone. Antonio said they didn't need help, but she went above his head and talked to his mom about it. I've also gone in a couple of times to pitch in, but Libby seems to have it under control. Mrs. Moretti adores her, which I think annoys the crap out of Antonio.

"It's fine." She shrugs, then fiddles with her hair.

That's something she's done since she was little—whenever she's not telling the truth.

"Just *fine?*" I narrow my eyes at her, and she shifts in her seat.

"*Just* fine."

"Is Antonio being nice to you?" I ask.

She rolls her eyes at the mention of his name.

"He's being himself."

"What does that mean?"

"It means he's constantly complaining about my shoes, my clothes, and the fact that I wear makeup."

"Don't let him get to you."

"I won't," she says, but I can tell by the set of her shoulders that his opinion bugs her.

"I'm sorry that he's being a jerk."

"Don't be. His opinion of me doesn't matter." She waves my comment away. "I like his mom, and his dad is very sweet. So he can suck it." She stands up. "I'm going to take a bath then watch a movie. Do you want to watch a scary one with me?"

"I'll make popcorn," I answer.

Watching her walk off toward our bedroom, I can't help but wonder what the hell is going on between her and Antonio. Her reaction was not normal. They have always bickered, but now I wonder if there isn't a little bit of attraction between them.

My cell phone starts to ring, and I lean forward and grab it off the coffee table.

It's Wesley. "Hey," I answer when I put it to my ear.

"Hey."

"Did you get your mom and Peter settled?" I ask as I relax back against the couch. Tucking my feet under me, I pull a blanket over my lap and get comfortable.

"Yeah. Now I'm heading to the station to meet Levi. We have to work for a few hours."

"Is everything okay?"

"Yeah, just work," he answers.

I know by his tone that he's not going to say anything more about it.

"I miss you," I say.

There's silence on the other end.

"Do you?" he asks after a moment.

I can hear the smile in his voice, which just makes me miss him even more.

"Yeah."

"I miss you, too."

"That makes me feel a little less crazy," I admit, smiling, then smiling wider when he laughs.

"My mom is crazy about you."

"She is?"

"She is. I knew she would be. She said that she loves you for me. That she couldn't have chosen better herself."

"That's good, right?" I ask, feeling hopeful.

"That's better than good. She's looking forward to meeting your family on Christmas."

"Oh." I deflate, slumping back into the couch. "Let's not get our hopes up, then. You and I both know that my family is crazy. She might change her mind about me after meeting them."

"It will be fine." He laughs, then I hear a car door slam.

"Did you just get to work?"

"Yeah, baby. I'll call you in the morning."

"Be safe."

"Always. Night, gorgeous."

"Night." I hang up, then press the cell phone to my smiling lips.

"What are you so happy about?" Libby asks, coming out of the bedroom wearing a robe. Her hair is tied up in a bun on top of her head.

"Wesley's mom likes me."

"Are you really surprised by that?" she asks, going to the kitchen.

She grabs a wineglass, then opens the fridge and pulls out a bottle of white wine, filling the glass to the brim.

"I don't know. I didn't know what to expect, honestly."

"Everyone likes you. Even Miss Ina, who I'm pretty sure hates everyone. So I'm not surprised." She takes a sip of wine, then holds the bottle up between us. "You want a glass?"

"No, thanks." I shake my head and she nods, putting the bottle back in the fridge. "Did you already take a bath?"

"Not yet. I'm filling the tub now. I just wanted a glass of wine."

"Cool." I yawn, covering my mouth. Then I reach forward for the remote. "If I'm asleep when you get out, just wake me up."

"Will do." She heads into the bedroom.

I turn on the TV and lie down, then promptly fall asleep.

When Libby does come out and wake me up, I'm only able to make it halfway through the movie *The Ring*. I can't keep my eyes open, so I give in and go to bed.

～

"Good morning!" Fawn says in a singsong voice as she walks into the apartment without knocking, making me jump out of my skin.

"Sheesh! You scared the crap out of me." I hold my hand over my pounding heart.

She smiles. "Sorry. I didn't even think twice about using my key." She shrugs, then holds up a bag. "I brought bagels."

My stomach, which has been silent all morning, growls. My mouth waters when I see the all-too-familiar name printed on the bag.

"Please tell me that you brought smoked salmon cream cheese," I beg, forgetting all about being scared moments ago.

"I did!" She smiles and sets the bag on the counter.

Pulling out the toaster, I plug it in, then dig out one of the "everything" bagels from the bag and cut it in half.

"You're here already," Libby says groggily, coming out of the bedroom.

Fawn looks at her when she comes over to kiss her cheek.

"Levi was out all night. He came in early this morning, so when he came to bed I got up so I wouldn't bother him," Fawn explains.

Libby makes her way past me and toward the coffeepot that finished brewing moments ago.

"Levi's already back to work?" Libby asks.

"Last night was his first night back. The doctors told him that as long as he doesn't push it, he should be okay."

"I haven't talked to Wesley this morning yet. Do you know if everything went okay last night?" I ask.

Fawn's face softens as she looks at me.

"Yeah, last night they got a lead that they needed to look into."

"Does Levi talk to you about his cases?" I ask, wondering if it's only Wesley who keeps his work from me.

"Never." She shakes her head as she accepts a cup of coffee from Libby. "I don't even ask him anymore. He knows if he needs to talk that I'm here for him, but he doesn't talk to me about work. Does Wesley talk to you?"

"No." I bite the inside of my cheek. Maybe I should ask my mom if my dad talked to her about work.

"I don't think you'd really *want* him to talk to you about his work," Libby says, wrapping her arm around my shoulder while taking a sip of coffee. "I love horror flicks, but I know there is no way that I would be able to handle seeing someone who was really murdered—or hearing about it firsthand." She shakes her head, then reaches around me to grab the bag of bagels. She pulls one out. "I think them not talking to you about work is their way of protecting you from how ugly the world is."

"Who protects *them*?" Fawn asks as my bagel pops up. "I love that Levi wants to protect me, but I also want to know that he's not carrying around the weight of everything he sees and does on his shoulders."

"I think you do that for him," I tell her honestly. "He may not talk to you about his job, but I don't think he needs to. I think you're his escape from all that."

"Exactly," Libby agrees, handing me a plate from the cupboard above the sink.

Grabbing a butter knife, I open the tub of smoked salmon cream cheese and slather a thick layer on my bagel. There is nothing better than New York City bagels and cream cheese. Nothing.

"So what stores are we hitting up first?" Libby asks.

I know she's excited about today. She's a marathon shopper; I swear that after shopping with her for one day, I need the rest of the year to recover. Today is the one day of the year when she can willingly get Fawn and me out of the house to shop with her. It's going to be crazy since today and the next two days are the craziest shopping days of the year. Everyone is out, and the stores are crowded, making it almost impossible to even move. Why we don't shop before today like most people, I don't know.

"I need to find something for Levi. I have no idea what to get him," Fawn says as she picks up the second half of my bagel and takes a bite.

"Lingerie," Libby says before taking a bite of her own bagel.

"Isn't that more of a gift for me than him?" Fawn frowns.

"No." Libby snorts, then asks, "Do you even *own* any lingerie?"

"No." She frowns.

"Well, then, tell me who would it be for?"

"Him, I guess." She shrugs.

"Exactly. It would be for him."

"I'll think about it."

"First stop, Victoria's Secret!" Libby says.

I wonder if I should go with her idea, too, because I have no idea what to get Wesley. What do you get the guy you've only been seeing for a few weeks? I don't even know if I should get him anything.

"I don't know what to get Wesley, either," I say.

Libby chews the bite she just took of her bagel, then swallows.

"What part of lingerie do you not understand? It's the gift that keeps on giving. You don't even need to tell him that it's a gift; he will just know when he unwraps it," she says.

I laugh. "Who the hell is unwrapping your gifts?"

"No one. I unwrap my own gifts, and I'm damn good at it, too." She winks.

I shake my head as Fawn laughs. "I miss you guys."

"I miss you, too. We need to have a set night every other week for sister time," I agree.

When we all lived together, we made it a point to have dinner together at least two nights a month. We would order in pizza or Chinese food, then lounge around in our PJs and watch scary movies until the early hours of the morning. When Fawn moved out, we let that tradition go, but I want to do that again. I miss how close we used to be.

"Yes, well, that is *if* your men will let you up for air long enough to hang out," Libby huffs.

I look at her just in time to catch her rolling her eyes.

"You sound a little jealous," Fawn states, smiling.

"Did I not just tell you how good I am at unwrapping myself? I'm so jealous I'm green. I want a man. A real living, breathing man." She tosses her hair.

"What about Antonio?" Fawn asks.

I turn to look at Libby.

"No, thank you. He's way too pompous for my taste."

"I don't know . . . when I was in there the other day to pick up my order and saw you two together, your arguing seemed a lot like foreplay."

"If foreplay is plotting someone's death in your mind from start to finish, including getting rid of the body, then you would be right," she says.

I know she's full of it. She's attracted to him, and it probably makes her crazy that he isn't falling at her feet like most men do. Libby is beautiful in a timeless way that calls to men, but most people don't know that she's a hard worker, she's ambitious, she's outgoing, and she's one of the kindest women I have ever met. Most men just see a pretty face and a perfect body—one that she does absolutely nothing to make that way. She eats like crap and never works out; if I ate like her, I would weigh five hundred pounds.

"All right, you two need to get ready so we can go. Times Square is going to be insane," Fawn says.

I shove the rest of my bagel in my mouth, chew, and swallow. I drink the rest of my coffee, then head to my room and get ready to spend the day with my sisters.

~

Sliding into a booth at the back of Jack's bar, across from my sisters, I smile at Libby and Fawn as they chat about all the things they bought. Pulling my eyes from them, I look around and realize I haven't been to Jack's in forever. The last time I was here was at Halloween with my sisters. Jack's has always been my favorite bar. I love the TVs in every corner playing different sports games, the worn tables that have dings and dents in them, and the crowd of men and women who are all there to have a good time.

"It's been a while, Mac," says Lisa, one of the waitresses, as she comes over to our table to drop off the drinks that we ordered when we first walked in.

I turn to look up at her and notice then that she's pregnant.

"Are you guys ready to order, or do you need a few minutes to look over the menu?"

"You're having a baby!" I blurt out.

She laughs, resting both her hands on her very round stomach.

"I'm so happy for you!" I get up and give her a hug. She hugs me back before letting me go and shaking her head.

"Yeah, me and Vick are so excited. I didn't know I was pregnant until two months ago. I thought I was just gaining weight." She laughs again, and I laugh along with her.

"That's great. Tell Vick I said congrats," I mutter, feeling a weight settle down around me.

I don't know what I would do if I found out I was pregnant right now. As good as things are between us, I don't know how Wesley would feel.

"Anyway, enough about me. Are you girls ready to order?" she asks.

"I think we're ready," Fawn says.

Libby and I both nod. We always get the same thing when we come here. I will have to work out for a week after this, but it's always worth it.

"Three cheeseburgers and fries, an order of cheese sticks, and an order of fried pickles."

"Sure," Lisa agrees.

My stomach twists.

"I'll bring your food out as soon as it's done."

"Thanks!" we say in unison before she walks off.

"Why do you look so pale?" Libby asks as soon as Lisa is gone.

I don't even know how to answer her. I don't know if I should just tell them that I messed up and had unprotected sex.

"Earth to Mackenzie!" Libby snaps her fingers in front of my face, and I blink.

"Wesley and I have had a couple accidents," I say.

My sisters share a look before they both frown at me.

"What does that mean?"

"We've had sex without protection."

"Seriously?" Libby hisses, leaning across the table toward me. "What the hell were you thinking?"

"I obviously *wasn't* thinking. But in my defense, the second he touches me, all rational thought goes out the window and I lose my mind. I know that it's stupid, but it's the truth. I swear I can't help myself around him."

"If you end up pregnant—" Fawn says, but I cut her off.

"I know," I whisper. "Believe me, I know. I've got a prescription for birth control, but I have to wait for my period to start this month to begin taking it."

"Well, you know Mom would be thrilled," Fawn laughs.

I cover my face and groan. Our mom *would* be thrilled if I got pregnant. She would think she hit the mother lode. With Fawn and me both in serious relationships and me pregnant, she'd probably faint from sheer happiness.

"What's the chance of it happening? I mean, it has to be like one in a million, right?" I ask.

Fawn shrugs, but Libby seems to ponder the question before giving her answer.

"I don't know. It's probably a lot more likely than you think it is. But then again, who the hell knows? There are a million variables that go into getting pregnant. Some women have to use thermometers, calculators, and calendars in order to get knocked up. Let's just hope you're like one of those women and not as fertile as Mom."

"Yeah, every time Mom said she wanted to have another baby, she got pregnant. So if you're anything like her, you're probably already carrying our niece or nephew," Fawn says, looking at my stomach.

I cover it with a hand without thinking, then quickly drop it away.

"Shut up and don't curse me! I don't even know what I would do if I ended up pregnant. And Wesley . . ." I shake my head. "I can't even imagine having to tell him that news. He would probably lock me in a room or roll me up in bubble wrap."

"Remind me why that's a bad thing?" Libby says, smiling at Lisa when she drops off our food at the table.

"It's not a bad thing. His crazy possessiveness gives me tingles, but it's annoying when he's overbearing. It's hard to explain—I love it but hate it."

"I get it," Fawn says, taking a sip from her wineglass. "Levi is a little cray-cray, too, but I try not to let him get away with it. I don't want him to think it's okay to boss me around or control me."

"Exactly. It's like a game of tug-of-war. He pushes, I pull, then he pushes again," I say, sliding my glass of wine across the table.

"I think I'll stick to loving myself. All this relationship business sounds way too complicated," Libby mutters.

Fawn laughs.

"It *is* complicated," I agree, wondering if it might become even more complicated.

Chapter 9

No Free Milk

Wesley

"Why on earth would a man want to buy the cow when he can just get the milk for free?" Miss Ina asks Mackenzie.

I see a smile twitch in the corner of my girlfriend's mouth. Libby, who has been attempting to get a rise out of the old lady since we sat down to Christmas dinner, tips her head to the side and puts on a look that's way too innocent.

"How will they know if the milk's not spoiled if they don't test it out?" Libby asks.

Miss Ina huffs.

Swallowing down a chuckle of my own, I look at my mom. She's sitting across from us, and I can see her shoulders shaking as she laughs silently.

When we arrived at the house and she was introduced to everyone, all my anxiety melted away. I should have known better than to be worried. There is no way Katie Reed would make anyone in her house feel uncomfortable. She made my mom and stepdad feel at home, and so did everyone else.

If I'm honest, today has been nice. When my parents divorced, there were no longer big holiday dinners with lots of family. It was mostly me with my dad on Christmas Eve, then with my mom on Christmas Day. Just us. Always just us. My mom didn't have any family, and my dad's family wanted nothing to do with my mom.

"Child, a man knows everything he needs to know about a woman the very moment they meet," Miss Ina says. "You don't need to give your milk away for him to know more. I met my late husband on a Monday and married him that Friday. He knew. We both knew what we were to each other—without any kind of taste test."

I cough into my hand to cover my laugh.

"That's amazing, Miss Ina, but the world is a different place now. Dating nowadays isn't like it used to be," Libby tells her truthfully. "Most people my age want casual relationships until they feel they are ready to start a family. Now most people I know don't date seriously unless they are looking to have a child, and then they are only looking for someone they believe will be a good parent, not necessarily a good partner."

"Bawww," Miss Ina says loudly, tossing out her hand. "You kids and all your fancy gadgets. You're always twittering, matching, and farmering."

"Farmering?" Libby repeats.

I wonder what the hell farmering is.

"Just yesterday, I saw an ad trying to recruit women to be farmers' wives on the television. What is this world coming to?" She shakes her head as her lip curls up in disgust. "You kids are so caught up in those gadgets you carry around in your hands that you don't even notice what's right in front of you anymore."

"That's very true," my mom agrees, nodding her head. "But Libby is also right. Dating nowadays isn't what it used to be." She picks up her wineglass to take a sip. "Even at my age, it was hard finding someone who wanted more than just a hookup."

"What is a hookup?" Miss Ina asks, frowning.

Libby leans to her side, "whispering" loud enough for everyone to hear. "It's another way of saying that you're giving your milk away for free."

"I know that, girl." Miss Ina glares at Libby, who smiles.

When we first got into the car that morning, I could tell that Libby didn't know what to think of Miss Ina. I don't know what changed, but about halfway to Long Island, something did. She started giving the older woman a hard time—and has clearly gotten a kick out of getting a rise out of her since then.

"We didn't 'hook up' in my day. We didn't live with each other for fun. We didn't play house. We met, we got married, we moved in together, and we had kids. Then we stayed married until the day one of us died."

"I'm glad it's not like that anymore," Libby says, looking around the table. "I know some people were happy, but there had to be a lot of people, a lot of women, who were unhappy and unable to do anything about it because society would have cast them out."

Miss Ina shrugs. "You're probably right, but this hooking-up business is not how you find someone you want to spend your life with. If you are constantly looking for the next hookup, as you say, you won't know when you find the right one."

"You're probably right," Libby agrees.

"I know I am. You and your sisters are sweet girls. You deserve to find nice men who want more than just to drink your milk."

Hearing Mackenzie snort next to me, I look at her just in time to catch her covering her mouth. "Sorry." She waves her hand toward Miss Ina, who narrows her eyes.

"This is the weirdest conversation I have ever heard," Levi says, picking up his beer.

Fawn smiles at him, resting her hand on his chest—a hand that is now sporting an engagement ring. When he told me a week ago that he was going to ask Fawn to marry him at Christmas, my first insane thought was that he was a lucky bastard. A few months ago, my first thought would have been that he was a crazy fuck.

Mackenzie has made me want those things for myself—a wife, a family, someone to come home to at the end of the day. She's my best friend. A best friend I have unbelievable chemistry with.

"Put down your darn phone, girl." I look up just in time to catch Miss Ina snatch the cell phone out of Libby's hand and toss it behind her onto the floor.

"You . . . oh my god! You did not just do that! I was posting a photo of what the table looked like after we all decimated it!" Libby cries.

Miss Ina waves her off. "You can't live life through a phone. You need to live in the moment by being *present* in the situation."

She isn't wrong about that. People now live on their phones. They date on their phones, communicate with family and friends on their phones. Face-to-face contact has become almost nonexistent.

"Yeah, but I wanted to share with my friends online who aren't here to share it with me."

"Share it with them firsthand when you see them. Not by taking a picture of the moment and sharing it on your Facesbooks or Intergrams," she says.

I smile at that.

"It's Facebook and Instagram. I don't see the people I chat with online often," Libby says.

Miss Ina frowns. "Then why do they need to see what your table looked like?"

"I don't know. It's just what you do. You share online what you're doing and where you have been."

"Well, it's ridiculous, and it takes away from the occasion and the experience. When you're enjoying a beautiful moment in life, really enjoying that moment, you can remember it in your mind's eye years later. You can remember what you heard, what you smelled, how you felt. Sometimes the memory will be so clear you'd think you were back there all over again. No picture is going to give that to you. If you don't put down your phone and look around, when you're old like me and your sight is starting to go, you will have no memories at all."

"You're right," Libby huffs. "But you still shouldn't have tossed my phone."

"You can get it after dinner," Miss Ina says before looking over at a stunned Katie, who is holding her glass of wine inches from her mouth. "Thank you for dinner, dear."

"Um . . ." Katie clears her throat. "You're welcome. Thank you for coming." She looks around the table. "Would anyone like dessert?" she asks, setting down her wineglass and standing up.

"I'd like some." Mackenzie's dad rubs her hand.

She nods once, then gets up and wanders from the dining room toward the kitchen.

"I'm going to go help my mom," Mackenzie says.

"Sure." I kiss the side of her head, and she smiles.

She scoots back from the table and gets up. Both Fawn and Libby follow her. Sitting back in my chair, I put my beer to my mouth and take a pull. Things are not at all uncomfortable, but Mackenzie's dad hasn't been his happy, talkative self since we got here. I can feel his strange energy coursing through the room like an exposed live wire. I don't know what's going on with him, but I think that Levi can feel it, too.

"I'm going to go have a smoke," my mom says.

I look at her and lift my chin.

"I'll go with you," Miss Ina says, pushing back her chair.

My mom looks at her with a surprised look on her face. "You smoke?"

"Not anymore, but I did years ago. You can blow it in my direction for old time's sake," she says.

Mom laughs as she and Miss Ina leave the room.

"That old lady is crazy," Peter mutters.

Levi and I both laugh, but Aiden doesn't. He crosses his arms over his chest and glares at Levi.

"You and I have some talking to do, boy," he says.

Levi holds up his hand in front of him. "I know. I didn't ask you in person about marrying her, but I swear there was no time. I had it in my head that I would ask her later on today, but when I woke up this morning I knew I wouldn't be able to sit with the ring in my pocket all day. That's why I called instead."

"You should have asked me in person," Aiden says, looking disappointed.

"I know, and I'm sorry." Levi runs his good hand through his hair. "You're right. I should have asked you in person."

Aiden looks at me, and I shift in my chair.

"If you're planning on asking Mac to marry you, you better heed my warning. Come ask me in person. I better not get a phone call from you at one in the morning," he says, looking back at Levi. "I wasn't happy about that call. When you guys have daughters, you'll under-stand how important it is."

I make a mental note to tell him about my intent to propose to Mac in advance.

"I'll remember that," I say.

He grunts, glaring at Levi once more. Then he smiles at the girls as they come back into the dining room carrying pies and plates.

"Is everything okay?" Mac whispers as she takes her seat next to me.

"Everything is fine," I assure her as her eyes take in the empty chairs across the table.

"What happened to your mom and Miss Ina?"

"They went out to smoke."

"Miss Ina *smokes?*" Libby asks as she takes her seat once more.

"No, but she wanted my mom to blow the smoke in her face for old time's sake," I say.

She shakes her head. "That lady is crazy."

"I heard that, girl," Miss Ina says as she comes back into the room followed by my mom.

Libby rolls her eyes. "Good," she mutters under her breath.

"I also heard *that*."

"I think Lib just found a new best friend," Mac whispers.

I laugh as Libby grouches something else under her breath that I can't make out.

Taking a bite of pie, I sit back and enjoy the quiet hum of conversation and laughter.

When it's time to go, I wish I didn't have to.

～

"Well, today was fun," Mom says as the town car pulls to a stop outside my apartment to let her and Peter off. Since Libby decided to stay out on Long Island with her parents, she suggested Mac take her bed and I take Mackenzie's so I won't have to sleep on the couch again at my place. I've learned the hard way over the last few days that it's less comfortable than I thought it was when I purchased it after moving here. I would much rather sleep in my bed with Mac, but I'll take what I can get.

"It was fun." Mac gets out to hug my mom on the sidewalk. "We will be back in the morning for breakfast."

"Sure thing." Mom kisses her cheek, then gives me a hug and a kiss. Peter gives Mac a hug.

Watching them head toward my apartment and disappear down the steps, I wait until I see a beam of light appear inside, then disappear behind them as the door closes. I get back into the car with Mac.

"You two better not keep me up all night, banging around," Miss Ina blurts into the quiet of the car. I fight back a laugh. I almost forgot that the old woman was still with us.

"Miss Ina, we're only going to sleep. You don't need to worry about us disturbing your slumber."

Mac sighs, so I give her knee a squeeze.

"Good. This world is going to hell in a handbag," she huffs, crossing her arms over her chest as she looks out the window.

"Maybe we should find you a boyfriend, Miss Ina," Mackenzie suggests, pulling out her phone. "They have a dating app for older people."

"Have you lost your mind, child? Does it look like I would ever need to find male companionship with the help of a telephone?" She crosses her arms over her chest again.

"Put like that, I guess not!" Mackenzie laughs.

"The day the portable phone was invented, the human IQ must have dropped ten points," Miss Ina mutters.

"Hey, that's not very nice."

"No, it's not nice. But it's the truth," she replies as the car pulls to a stop in front of Mackenzie's building.

"Whatever . . . ," Mackenzie grumbles back.

Shaking my head at the two of them, I open the door. I get out, then help both women out of the backseat. I take Miss Ina's arm and help her up the steps to the front door. She refused to bring her walker with her today. Even though she's been getting around pretty well, I did notice that later on in the evening she started favoring her right leg more than her left—showing that she's in pain, even if she would never admit it. Once we're inside the house, Mackenzie takes over helping the older woman. I open the door to Miss Ina's apartment and let both women in.

"Thank you. Even though you didn't exactly give me much of a choice, I had a very nice time today," Miss Ina says.

Mackenzie kisses her wrinkled cheek and helps her get settled on the couch.

"You're welcome to come with us tomorrow for breakfast," I invite her, knowing that she's alone.

"No, you two enjoy yourselves. I'm going to spend the day at home, resting."

"Are you sure?" Mackenzie asks, taking her walker over to the couch and setting it up right in front of her.

"Yes, dear." Miss Ina pats her cheek.

"All right, Miss Ina," Mackenzie agrees.

She takes my hand and leads me toward the door.

"Have a good night."

"You too!" Miss Ina calls out as we leave.

Heading up the stairs to Mackenzie's place, I watch her ass move in the high-waisted slacks she has on. Slacks that are molded to the dip of her waist and the flare of her hips and ass that I wouldn't mind biting.

"Did you have fun tonight?" she asks.

I pull my eyes from her ass to catch her smiling at me from the top step.

"It was nice," I say.

She laughs, putting her hand against my chest. "We are not having sex, mister. Did you not hear Miss Ina? She doesn't want to listen to us getting it on, and believe me, she would hear it. You can't be quiet enough to get it past her."

"What about in the shower?" I ask, pressing against her back as she unlocks the door to her apartment.

She looks at me over her shoulder. I watch her pupils dilate, then her tongue comes out, touching her bottom lip.

"I don't think my shower is big enough for the two of us," she says before looking away from me, pushing the door open, and stepping inside.

She takes off her coat, and I shut the door before I take off my own jacket and toss it on the back of the couch. I take just a second to glance around.

"The walls seem solid."

"She'd still hear us."

"How do you know that?" I ask, feeling jealousy curl around my middle at the idea of her in here with another man and making the sounds I've come to crave from her.

"I know because Libby and I can hear the people upstairs from us getting it on all the time. We can hear them no matter where they are—in bed, in the shower, in the kitchen. We hear it all. So I know Miss Ina would hear us. Since she is just now starting to like me, I'm not going to jeopardize that for some penis."

"It's a big penis," I remind her, taking a step in her direction.

She takes a step back.

"It is a big penis, but until your mom and Peter leave, he and I are going to have to be penis pals," she says, making me chuckle as I back her up against the wall next to the front door.

"Penis pals? What kind of relationship is that?"

"Friends from afar." She rests her hand against my chest.

"I don't want to be friends from afar. What if I just use my mouth and leave my penis out of it?"

"I'd still want the penis at the end, so the answer is no."

"You love him?"

"I'm madly in love with your penis, but he needs to stay away from me tonight."

"What if I just use the tip?" I say.

She laughs hard, dropping her forehead to my shoulder, her body shaking.

"There is no way you could just stick in the tip and not try to fill me with your cock," she says to make me groan.

"Don't say 'cock' or remind me of what it's like when I fill you with it. He misses you too much. These last few days have been torture." I grind against her. "Let me eat your pussy, gorgeous. At least let me get a taste."

"Don't talk like that."

"Maybe I shouldn't ask at all. Maybe I should tie you up and just take it."

I kiss up her jaw to her ear, listening to her breathing turn into tiny, shallow pants. They are killing me slowly.

"Do you want that, gorgeous? Do you want me to take the choice away from you?"

"No," she whimpers as I unhook the button of her pants and zip them down.

"Are you wet?"

"You know I am."

"You're always wet for me, aren't you?"

"Yes." Her nails dig into my shoulders as I slide my fingers between her folds. She's drenched, and my mouth waters at the idea of getting it on her. "Wesley . . ."

"Yeah?"

"Please don't tease me."

Her head falls back, and I kiss down her neck.

"I don't plan on teasing you. Kick off your boots," I instruct.

She does, which makes her shrink a couple of inches. Unbuttoning her top, I slide it off her shoulders, then reach behind her and remove her bra, adding it to the growing pile on the ground.

"Miss Ina is going to be so mad at us," she breathes against my lips.

I want to growl that I don't give a fuck, but I know if I do she will shut this down.

"She won't even know." I help her out of her pants, then lead her over to the couch. "Kneel away from me, gorgeous."

"What are you going to do?" she asks, looking at me over her shoulder. Seeing her hair down, her mouth soft, and her big eyes, my dick throbs.

"You'll see." I help her onto the couch, then kneel down on the ground behind her. "Now, bend at the waist until your face is on the cushion. If you need to scream or moan, you do it into that cushion."

Cheeks pinking, she bends forward and her ass rises into the air. When I see her in that position, I have to remind myself that this is for her, not me—okay, so it's kinda for me, too. Taking hold of her hips, I blow across her wet sex and lean back to watch as goose bumps break out across her smooth skin.

"Fuck, I want inside you."

I run my fingers down her sex. Her hips buck before I follow my fingers with my tongue and lick up her center. "Remember, you need to be quiet," I remind her when she moans. I fight the urge to smack her ass. Rubbing it and grabbing a handful, I squeeze hard. "I want to spank you. I want to see my handprint on your skin. I want to feel you contract around my tongue when my hand makes contact. You want that, too, I know you do." I slip one finger inside of her, then another, pumping them slowly while tonguing her clit.

"Wesley . . ."

Her breath catches as she says my name, and I tighten my hold on her ass while speeding up my fingers to bring her closer to the edge. Feeling her thighs start to shake, I pull on her clit, sucking it and flicking it with my tongue. Hearing her scream into the couch cushion, I give her one final lick.

She shudders while whimpering.

Getting up off the floor, I take a seat on the couch and pull her into my lap before adjusting her against my chest. Pushing her hair out of her face, I kiss her forehead, then each of her eyelids and her lips.

"Are you okay?"

"I think so." She smiles up at me from under her lashes before letting them slide closed once more. "I miss sleeping in your arms." She snuggles closer, pressing her nose against my chest.

As her breathing changes and her body relaxes against mine, I study her. Even with all the time we've been spending together the last few weeks, I still don't know which girl she is, the sexy siren I had sex with the night we met, or the woman who can talk about baseball like she works for the Mets. Then again, I don't think I want to know. I like the idea of trying to figure her out for the rest of our lives. I like that she will maybe always be a little bit of a mystery to me.

Dropping my lips to her forehead, I hold them there and whisper, "I think I love you, Mackenzie Reed, and it scares the shit out of me."

Chapter 10

Tiny Human

Mac

Pregnant, pregnant, pregnant. Pregnant, pregnant. I look at the five tests on the counter. Five different brands of tests, and they all say the same thing: I'm pregnant.

"Holy shit." I lean back against the wall, then slide down until my ass hits the floor. I let my legs sprawl out in front of me as I stare at the bathroom door.

"There is a tiny human growing inside of me." I press the palms of my hands against my stomach and close my eyes. I don't know what the hell I'm going to do. I don't know how I'm going to tell Wesley this news.

When I didn't get my period a week ago, I knew I needed to take a test, but I kept putting it off and putting it off. Libby tossed a test at me this morning before she left for work, reminding me that if I wanted to have a drink tonight, on New Year's Eve, I needed to make sure I wasn't pregnant. Guess there will be no drinking for me.

"Mac?" Libby yells through the bathroom door.

I close my eyes. When I took that first one and it came back positive, I went out and got a few more, thinking the first one was a fluke. Apparently it wasn't—unless there is something wrong with my pee.

"Mac!" Libby calls again.

"Give me a minute!" I shout back.

She doesn't listen. The pocket door slides open, and she sticks her head into the room and looks around until she finds me sitting on the floor.

"What are you doing?"

"Just hanging out. It's a nice room. I'm thinking about moving my bed in here," I say as she looks at me.

Then she spots all the tests lined up on the counter.

"You're . . ."

"Pregnant, with a tiny human." I finish her sentence.

She comes into the room and takes a seat on the toilet, resting her elbows on her knees.

"There is a human person growing inside of me. Like the movie *Alien*, only it's not an alien—it's a baby."

"You're going to be a mom!" She cuts off my rambling.

My heart seizes up. "I'm going to be a mom." I close my eyes, the reality really hitting me. I don't just have a human growing inside of me; I have a human growing inside of me that is part of me and part of Wesley. Our child. A tear tracks down my cheek, and an unbelievable amount of love fills every single cell in my body. "What if he doesn't want this?"

"Stop being dumb." She smacks my upturned knee. "You are his cow, his milk-mate."

"You seriously need to stop spending so much time with Miss Ina." I scrub my hands down my face to wipe away the tears that have fallen.

"The news might shock him, but once it settles in, he's going to be fine. My guess is he's even going to be a little excited."

"Why do you say that?" I grab some tissue and wipe under my eyes.

"Because I see the way he looks at you. He's always watching you like he's just waiting for something to happen so that he can jump in and save you. It's the same way Dad looks at Mom and Levi looks at Fawn," she says.

I really, really hope she's right.

"This is going to change everything."

"Yep." She picks up another test off the counter and looks at it. "You're pregnant with my niece or nephew! I'm going to be an aunt!"

"A baby." The idea is so overwhelming and exciting. I'm scared out of my mind, but I also cannot wait. It's like waiting in line for an amusement park ride—you know it's going to be scary, but thrilling at the same time.

"I call godmother!" she blurts.

I pull my eyes off my stomach to look at her.

"You can't 'call' godmother. It's not the front seat of a car; it's my child."

"So who are you going to pick, then?"

"I don't know. Maybe Wesley will want to choose someone."

"Fine. I'm going to tell him that I call godmother," she mutters.

I roll my eyes at her.

"How are you going to tell him the news?"

"I don't know. Maybe I should just wait until after I see the doctor. What if the tests are wrong?"

"I don't think five tests could be wrong, so I don't think you need to worry about that. But if you think you need to wait a little before telling him, I get that. I just wouldn't wait too long. You don't want it to turn into you keeping the news from him. If he finds out that you've known for a long time and not told him, that's how he's going to feel. Like you were hiding it from him."

"You're right. I'll tell him tomorrow," I say, then shake my head. "Or after the weekend."

I need more time to process, and I do want to see a doctor before I tell him, just to be sure.

"Mom is going to freak. She was excited about Fawn getting married, and now you have just blown *that* news out of the water. The only way this could be any better is if you're pregnant with twins."

"Shut up." The idea alone makes me panic. I've barely wrapped my head around the idea of one baby—I don't know what I would do with two.

"Just reminding you that they do run in our family . . ."

She grins, and I smack her knee.

"You are so evil!" I laugh, and she stands and then helps me up.

"Come on. I want to show you the dress I got for you."

"Is it anything like our Halloween dresses from a few months ago?" I ask.

She grins. "No, and I didn't pick those out. You did."

"I know."

I shake my head at the reminder of how stupid I was. On Halloween, I decided that I would once and for all get Edward—aka Sir Dick the Cheater—to notice me by dressing up with my sisters for a Halloween party at Jack's. We went as prostitutes, and that was where things started to go downhill. Our coats got stolen, the second thing that happened, then what topped it all off was getting stopped by the police because they thought we were really prostitutes.

"Are you ready?" Libby asks, bringing me out of my thoughts.

I blink. Seeing the navy-blue, floor-length, V-neck lace dress lying across the bed, I gasp. It's perfect, so perfect. Wesley is going to freak out when he sees me in it. Most officers are working tonight, but Wesley got off so that he could attend a New Year's Eve charity ball with me. Jack's hosts it every year. The money raised tonight will be donated to a children's baseball charity that Jack's runs to provide inner-city kids with training, uniforms, and travel expenses. I love it, and I love the cause.

"It's perfect," I whisper, running my hand down the soft material.

"Duh." Libby nudges my shoulder. "I'm good at what I do."

"You really are good. Thank you so much for this."

"You know, it's not a big deal."

"It *is* a big deal."

A couple of years ago, Libby started up a little side business. She basically rents out items from other people's closets. Things that can be worn only once by the owner, like the dress on the bed. The person renting the item puts down a large deposit before receiving the dress, then after she wears it, she returns it to Libby, who has the item cleaned and returns it to its original owner, like new. I haven't asked her how much she's made so far, but I know that she's been somewhat successful with her new venture.

"I say we do your hair up and to the side. Your makeup needs to be dramatic."

"You can do whatever you want," I tell her.

She raises a brow at me. "Anything?"

"Anything." I wiggle my brows back.

"You never let me do whatever I want."

"Well, tonight is your night. My only stipulation is that you make me look beautiful."

"I don't need to make you beautiful. You already are beautiful."

My face softens.

"I'm just going to make you look like a sex goddess."

I smile when she says this. "This sex goddess needs a shower first." I walk past her toward the bathroom, asking, "So what are *your* plans for the night?"

"I told Antonio I would come in and help him out since it's New Year's Eve. I will most likely ring in the new year covered in flour and smelling like pizza."

"Have things been better between you two?"

"We don't really talk. He grunts at me every once in a while, but for the most part we don't speak," she says, sounding disappointed.

I tip my head to the side to study her.

"You like him," I say.

She shrugs. "A little, but it doesn't matter. He will never see me as anything more than a pretty face, and I will probably always think he's a Neanderthal."

"But—"

"No." She cuts me off before I can convince her that maybe she's wrong. "Go shower before I change my mind about doing your hair and makeup." She shoves me back toward the bathroom, then closes the door, leaving me no choice but to drop it.

~

"Holy shit."

The look in Wesley's eyes when I open the door lets me know that the last few hours of torture have been so worth it. After showering, and shaving everything, Libby spent an ungodly amount of time blowing out my hair. Then she spent an even longer amount of time curling it before putting it in a crazy updo that is being held together by at least a thousand bobby pins. If there is a metal detector at the door tonight, I know I will set it off. After she finally finished my hair, she did my makeup similar to the way she did it the night Wesley and I met— smoky and mysterious. The makeup and hair both look amazing, but the dress . . . the dress is everything. The dark blue looks fabulous with my red hair and fair skin, and the cut is beyond sophisticated and sexy. I look classy and hot, if I do say so myself.

"Holy shit."

"You said that already." I smile.

His eyes travel from my feet back up to my cleavage. They pause there for a moment before he meets my gaze once more.

His eyes are so dark with desire that my breath catches.

"Holy shit," he repeats again.

I laugh.

"Gorgeous. You look . . ."

"She looks like a sex goddess," Libby says from my side.

Wesley looks at her, nodding and adjusting the tie around his neck.

"She does," he agrees. His eyes come back to me. "I don't know whether to show you off or hide you away." He wraps his hand around my hip and brings himself closer to me. "You look beautiful."

"Thank you." I tip my chin back to accept his kiss, then take hold of the lapels of his tux. "You look handsome. So very, very handsome."

"Okay, you both look great. As much as I want to stand here and watch the love fest you have going on, I need to leave, so you are going to have to stop blocking the door." Libby breaks into our moment.

I laugh, turning to watch her put on her jacket.

That's when I notice her feet. "What the hell are those?" I point to the Converse sneakers she has on.

"They're called shoes." She rolls her eyes.

I feel my own eyes widen. "*I* know that, but you don't wear sneakers. What the hell is going on?"

"Okay, drama llama, it's not a big deal. I need to wear sneakers since I'm going to be on my feet running around, answering phones, and waiting tables all night." She kisses my cheek, then Wesley's. "Have fun tonight!" she calls over her shoulder as she heads down the steps.

I watch her until she is out of sight.

"She *never* wears sneakers," I say out loud to myself.

"She's gonna be busy. She wants to be comfortable," Wesley says, walking me backward into my apartment. When he shuts the door, I snap out of my thoughts and blink at him.

"What are you doing?" I step away from him, but he steps closer again. "We have to go or we are going to be late."

"We won't be late."

"If you touch me, we will be late." I sidestep him, then grab my coat and slip it on. I tie the belt as tight as I possibly can and hold the ends so he can't rip it open.

"Just one little touch."

"You can touch me later." I grin at the pout he gives me. He looks like a little kid who's just been told he's not allowed to have more candy. "Come on." I take his hand to lead him out of the apartment but squeak as he picks me up, bride-style. "What are you doing?"

"Carrying you so that you don't break your neck on the way down the stairs. I want to be able to touch you tonight, and that will be impossible if you're in a full-body cast."

"Very funny." I tap his cheek after he sets me on my feet on the sidewalk outside. A cab is waiting for us. After helping me into the back and getting in with me, he gives the driver directions to our venue. Since it's New Year's Eve and there are so many roads blocked off, it takes a lot longer than normal to make it across the city.

Once we arrive at the event space, I take in its beauty. Cipriani's limestone architecture blends in with the rest of the buildings across from Grand Central. But what's inside makes it one of the most sought-after places for parties in the city. Jack and Vivian, the owners of Jack's, grew up with the owner of Cipriani's children, so every year they allow Jake to use the space for next to nothing when I'm sure it would normally cost tens of thousands of dollars for New Year's. Once we get inside, we stop at the coatroom and then make our way to the main room. Every year when I come here, the ballroom makes me want to take a trip to Rome to see the architecture there firsthand. I'm so in love with the marble columns that stretch up and up to the cathedral ceilings. The room screams elegance.

"Do you know where we're sitting?" Wesley asks as we move through the crowded room with my hand tucked in the crook of his arm.

"Elizabeth told me last night that I'm sitting with her and Tex," I tell him, looking around for my friends. I met Tex and Elizabeth at

Jack's. We bonded over our mutual love for the Mets and have been friends ever since.

"Do you see them?"

"No." I shake my head, scanning the room.

When I finally see them in the back, at a round table, my stomach turns. Tex and Elizabeth are sitting at a six-top table with Edward and Bonnie and two empty chairs. If the two chairs are really ours, I'll have to sit across from Bonnie the entire night without blurting out anything about Edward being a cheater. I need a drink—not that I can have one, but I need one. Then again, it's probably best that I can't drink because when I do drink, I tend to talk a lot. "I found our table," I tell Wesley, and I feel him tense when he sees where my eyes are pointing and who we will be sitting with.

"Are you going to be okay sitting at a table with him?" he asks, moving his hand to my lower back, then sliding it around to my hip so he can hold me closer.

"I think so, but I think we should make up a safe word," I whisper, looking up at him.

"A safe word?" He raises a brow. "What do you know about safe words?"

"Not much more than is explained in *Fifty Shades of Grey*," I admit.

His eyes change ever so slightly.

"You read those books?" he asks quietly, turning me to face him.

I look around, realizing that we are standing in the middle of the dance floor and that there are people all around us dancing.

"Yes." I shrug as his fingers dig into my hips.

"Well, things in the bedroom are about to become a little more interesting," he mutters.

My stomach does a flip, but I ignore it. I need to concentrate on what's happening right now. I can't let him sidetrack me.

"Focus." I smack my hands flat against his chest. "We need a safe word so if I start to feel like I can't keep it together any longer, if I can't keep myself from blurting out to Bonnie about Edward, I say the safe word and you get me out of there—pronto." I snap my fingers.

"Okay, what's the safe word?"

"I don't know . . ." I look around. "How about *octopus*?"

"So you're randomly going to blurt out *octopus*?" He raises one brow.

"When you say it like that, it sounds like a stupid idea." I sigh, and he laughs.

"How about you just say, 'I love this song, dance with me'?"

Tipping my head to the side, I study him, then ask, "Do you know how to dance?"

"Maybe." He kisses my nose. "You'll find out if we need to make an escape."

"Fine." I pull in a breath, then let it out. "I really hate the idea of sitting across from her and breaking bread knowing that her man is a dick."

"You're not Mafia, so you're not 'breaking bread' with her; you're sitting at a table with her at a charity event."

"Tomato, tomahto." I wave him off, and he smiles, then dips his head, kissing me.

"It will be fine. Now come on, I'm hungry." He puts my hand back in the crook of his arm before leading me across the room toward our table. We stop a few times to say hi to people I know so I can introduce Wesley to them.

When we make it to the table, Edward gets up and comes around the table to hug me. I feel Wesley tense up.

"You look amazing," Edward says against my ear before Wesley pulls me away from him. Giving his hand a reassuring squeeze, I turn toward Tex and Elizabeth.

"Hey, guys."

I greet them both with a hug, then introduce them to Wesley, whom they haven't met until today. While Wesley is busy talking with Tex, I turn to Bonnie.

"How are you?" I greet her with a smile and a hug.

She hugs me back and replies, "I've been good."

"Great." I take a step away from her. "I love your dress."

"Thank you." She runs her hands down the silky black material at her sides and hips. She really does look beautiful. It accents her long, dark-blonde hair perfectly, and her California tan makes her big blue eyes stand out.

"Elizabeth, seriously, you look amazing, too," I say to my friend.

Then I look up at Tex, who towers over her by at least a foot. "That dress shows off her long legs, and the red is beautiful on her. How hard was it for you to let her out of the house?"

"Hard." He grins. Tex and Elizabeth met on an airplane going to London from JFK. When they arrived in London, they spent a week together. When they came back to the States, Tex moved from Texas to New York to be with her, and they've been together ever since. And now they are working on Tex's football team—they've got three boys already, and a few weeks ago, Elizabeth told me that she's pregnant again. She keeps trying for a girl—and Tex just keeps trying because he secretly loves Elizabeth pregnant.

"Here, gorgeous." Wesley pulls out a chair for me, and I take a seat, then rest my hand on my own flat stomach. "You have that look I hate," he says close to my ear.

I turn to look at him. "What look?"

His fingers touch my chin, then run across my jaw. "The one that says you're about to run on me."

"I'm not going to run." I take his hand off my chin and twine our fingers together. "I promise."

"You better not."

"I won't." I smile and he leans in, kissing me softly.

Sitting back, I take a breath to steady myself. Bonnie's ring catches my attention, and I can't help but admire it again. It's beautiful, with one large, center diamond that's somewhat elevated above the rest of the stones that drip down the band.

"Isn't it beautiful?" Bonnie asks, holding it up.

I meet her gaze and nod, giving her a smile.

"It's really beautiful. He did a good job."

"I know." She turns her hand from side to side. "It's a little small, but Edward promised that when he makes his first million, he'll get me a new one."

"Oh . . ." I try not to frown.

Edward shifts like he's uncomfortable. Not that I can blame him. His fiancée just said that the ring he gave her isn't good enough. Maybe they deserve each other.

"So, Wesley, tell us a little about yourself. What do you do for a living?" Edward cuts in to break the awkward moment.

"I'm a detective with the NYPD," Wesley answers, sitting back and undoing the button on his tux jacket.

"He actually works with Fawn's fiancé, Levi," I explain, covering his hand with mine on the top of the table.

"Is that how you two met?" Elizabeth asks.

I feel a blush spread up my neck and cheeks.

"No, we actually met before we knew about that connection," I say.

She squints her eyes at me, and I shift uncomfortably.

"It seems like there is a story there. You need to come over for wine so you can fill me in on all the dirty details," Elizabeth says.

I smile at her. "I know! Plus, I need to see the boys—I haven't seen them in ages."

"We'll make a date."

"Gorgeous, dance with me." Wesley cuts into the conversation and stands suddenly. I tip my head back to look at him and instantly register the look on his face.

"We'll be back." I smile at everyone at the table as he pulls out my chair, then let him lead me out to the dance floor. I smile at the other couples, then rest both my hands against his chest and look up at him. "What's wrong?"

"Besides Edward looking at your tits every five seconds, that chick tried to feel me up under the table."

"What?" I shout, stopping in place. Looking around his shoulder and back toward the table, I narrow my eyes at Bonnie when our gaze locks.

Forcing me to move along with him, he holds me tighter. "The first time it happened, I thought it was an accident. Then it happened again."

"That's . . . that's . . . I don't know what that is. Rude just doesn't cover it."

I look over at the table again. Both Edward and Bonnie are looking at us, but Tex and Elizabeth are busy making googley-eyes at each other. Glaring at Bonnie, I see her frown before Wesley forces me to look at him.

"I can't believe that she would hit on you when I'm sitting *right there*."

"Don't think about it." He wraps his hand around my jaw, then lowers his mouth to mine. The kiss is soft and sweet, and it does exactly what I need it to—forget about everyone around us. When he pulls his mouth from mine, I smile. "Better?"

"Yes." I rest my temple to his shoulder. "I didn't know you knew how to dance."

"This isn't dancing; this is swaying. The moment they put on dance music, you'll see my moves."

"I can't wait." I laugh and close my eyes, swaying with him until it's announced that dinner is being served.

We go back to the table. Thankfully, Bonnie keeps her hands to herself, and the rest of the dinner goes by without incident. After dinner, we spend most of the night on the dance floor, where Wesley proves that he's not a liar. He *can* dance—and well.

Getting into the back of the cab a few hours later, I'm all danced out. I can't stop smiling.

"Did you have a good night, gorgeous?" Wesley asks after shutting the door.

"Yes, and I learned something new about you," I say as the cab pulls away from the curb and into traffic. "You are really good at dancing. If they ever have a *Dancing with the Stars* NYPD edition, I think you should try out."

I yawn, and he laughs and kisses the top of my head.

"I'll keep that in mind. Are you tired?"

"Very." I yawn again. He wraps his arm around my shoulder, and I snuggle into his side.

Suddenly, the cab is jolted forward, and my body is tossed against the partition that separates us from the driver. My head and knees hit it hard. Wesley's arm wraps around my waist, but a second impact comes, even worse than the first. He's unable to keep me in his grasp as the car is jolted again. Glass rains down around us from my window as it shatters. Grabbing my head, I feel wetness on my fingertips.

"Are you okay?" His eyes scan me, and I nod my head.

"I think so. But . . ."

"Fuck." He looks around, then settles me back against the seat. "Do not move." He opens his door and gets out. My knees ache and my head is pounding, but with all that, my biggest concern right now is our baby.

Our baby that Wesley doesn't know about.

"Wesley!" I call his name as he reaches into the backseat for me.

Helping me out, he looks me over once more, then inspects my forehead and the wound that is causing blood to run down my face and onto my chest and dress. Libby is going to kill me.

"Hold on, gorgeous. I want to get you safely across the street. Okay?" I shake my head no. "I promise it will be okay. I know you're bleeding, but it's just a small scrape. I promise, it's small." He picks me up and moves quickly through the cars that are now piled up in the middle of the road.

"Wesley . . ."

"Here you are." He heads toward a bench at an empty bus stop, then helps me sit.

From my new vantage point, I can see the full scene of the accident. Two cars hit our cab—one in the back and one on the side. The yellow cab is not just wrecked, it's totaled.

"Stay here. I'll be right back. Don't move. Just keep pressure on your head," he says, taking off his jacket and wrapping it around my shoulders.

"Wesley!" I repeat once more as he puts his cell phone to his ear.

"I'll be right back." He kisses my forehead, then stands.

Completely frustrated with him, I shout, "I'm pregnant!"

Even being in the middle of a busy intersection with police sirens off in the distance blaring as they race toward us, and people who have stopped on the sidewalks to take in the accident—even with all that, I know that if I had a pin to drop, I would have heard it. It was like the air went still, and all the people froze just like in those superhero movies when everything stops, even the bullets in midair.

Then time returns to normal and chaos ensues.

"Get a fucking ambulance, and get it here right fucking now!" Wesley shouts to whomever he's talking to on the phone; then he drops to his knees in front of me. "Are you okay? Are you hurting? Are you in any pain?"

"No pain, but what if the accident shook the baby loose?" I say, knowing rationally that that is ridiculous and impossible.

"I don't think that's possible, but when the ambulance gets here, I will have them check to make sure that didn't happen."

"Good." I pull in a sharp breath when his large palm reaches under my coat and covers my stomach.

"You're pregnant." It's not a question; I know he's just asking me to confirm what I just told him.

"Yes."

"With my baby . . . ," he says.

I narrow my eyes on his. "That better be a joke, because if it's not, I swear the moment I know I'm okay I'm going to kick your ass all over New York City."

"Gorgeous, shut up and kiss me," he demands.

So of course I do.

Chapter 11

OH, BABY, YOU'VE LOST YOUR MIND

WESLEY

Sitting in the hospital with my elbows on my knees and my head in my hands, I try to keep my shit together. Mackenzie is pregnant. She's pregnant with our child, and I could have lost her and the baby tonight. The idea of going through my life without Mackenzie is completely unbearable. I'm in love with her. Fuck. I feel happy as hell and sick to my stomach at the same time.

"Are you okay?"

Lifting my head, I look at Mackenzie. She's looking like she doesn't have a care in the world as she sits on the top of the table reading one of the ripped-up magazines that got left behind in the room by someone. When the ambulance showed up on the scene, I made sure they saw to her first. The wound on her head was superficial, like I thought, but they still used butterfly tape to close it up. She will have a bruise for a few days. Her knees are also black and blue from where they hit the divider, but they weren't causing her any kind of abnormal pain. They were most concerned with her losing the baby.

"Okay, mister. Snap out of it." She taps my cheek before carefully draping herself across my lap. I didn't even realize she had stood up.

"I'm all right." I adjust her, then rest my hand over her flat stomach. The idea of it growing with our child is overwhelming and unbelievable. I can't get my mind around the fact that I'm going to be a dad.

"You're such a liar." She sighs, resting her hand over mine on her stomach and dropping her head onto my shoulder. "We are not very good at being traditional, are we?"

Dipping my chin to see her face, I hate the worry I see there. "Have I told you today that I like you a lot?" I ask.

Her eyes meet mine, the worry slowly fading into something else that I like a lot more.

"No." She shakes her head.

Cupping her cheek, I smooth my thumb over the soft surface. "Actually, I think I'm in love with you."

"You do?" she whispers, searching my gaze.

"I do," I say, watching her smile a beautiful smile before resuming her previous position. Frowning, I give her a gentle squeeze. "Do *you*?"

"Do I what?" she asks.

I can't tell if she's joking or not. "Do you love me, woman?"

"Miss Reed?" The door opens and the doctor comes into the room before she can answer my question. I throw the doctor a dirty look—not that she notices. She's focused on the stack of papers in her hands. Easing Mackenzie off my lap, I help her back onto the table and stand next to her. "It's nice to meet you two." The doctor looks between us.

"You too." Mackenzie gives her a warm smile.

I grunt my greeting, still annoyed that we were interrupted moments ago.

"Stop it." Mackenzie hits my chest with the back of her hand, and the doctor looks between the two of us before continuing.

"Your blood test came back positive, so you are definitely pregnant."

I reach forward and take Mackenzie's hand when I see it start to shake.

"I also ordered an internal ultrasound so that we can just make sure that everything is okay. I don't predict that there will be a problem since you haven't had any bleeding or cramping. The baby should be okay," she says.

I let out a breath I didn't know I was holding. I knew that chances were that the baby was okay, but it's a relief to hear that from the doctor.

"So the accident didn't shake him loose?" Mackenzie says.

The doctor laughs. "No, it's pretty safe in there with all that cushioning. Fetuses are much more resilient than you think."

"Thank god." She covers her stomach with her hand, and I place my hand over hers.

"Now just hold tight for a few minutes. The ultrasound tech should be in to take you over to see the baby."

"Thank you."

"You're welcome. Here is my card. I work here in emergency a few nights a week, but I have a practice downtown with a few other doctors. If you're looking for prenatal care, give my office a call and they will set you up with an appointment."

"Awesome." Mackenzie takes the card, then hands it to me since she doesn't have a purse.

Tucking it into my wallet, I watch the doctor leave.

Once the door is closed, I turn to Mackenzie. "You didn't answer my question."

"What question?" She tips her head to the side.

If I didn't see the sparkle of amusement in her gaze, I would be offended.

"You are an evil woman," I growl, forcing her back onto the table.

Her hands slide through my hair.

"That's payback for asking if it's your baby," she says with a smile.

I wrap my hand around the lower part of her jaw and gently tilt her head back. I dip my face close to hers until we are sharing the same breath.

"Let's try this again. Mackenzie, I'm crazy in love with you." My thumb rubs across her smooth skin, and my eyes stay locked with hers. I see them fill with tears.

"I love you, too." Her eyes close, and I swipe away one lone tear that falls from under her lashes before placing my mouth against hers.

"Miss Reed, I'm ready for you. Just follow me," a woman says as she pokes her head into the room.

Mackenzie wipes the tears off her cheeks with jerky movements. Helping her sit up, I press one more quick kiss to her lips, then help her down off the table. Taking her hand, we head down the hall into another room, where a machine is set up next to a hospital bed.

"Panties off. Put this on. I'll be back in just a moment." The woman hands over a paper robe before leaving us alone in the room.

Kicking off her heels, she turns her back to me. "Can you help me out of my dress?"

Stepping up behind her, I undo the button at the top, then start to unzip the dress. It exposes inch after inch of creamy, freckled skin.

"This is not exactly the way I saw myself getting you out of this dress tonight." I kiss her shoulder, then the exposed skin of her back.

"It's not the way I thought it would be, either."

She shivers as I slide the dress off completely. I curse under my breath when I see the lace bra and panties she has on. A dark-blue lace the same color of her dress, sheer enough to show off her beautiful skin.

"I don't think you need to take off my bra." She laughs, taking a step away from me and my hands that had started to unhook the clasp of her bra.

"Habit."

I help her step out of the dress, then help her put on the paper robe. She slips off her panties before she gets onto the bed. Hearing a knock, I call, "Come in!"

The tech steps back in and dims the lights.

"Is this your first child?" she asks, moving to the machine on the opposite side of me and typing on the odd-looking keyboard.

"Yes," we both say at the same time.

I take Mackenzie's hand, and we listen to the woman explain exactly what she is going to do, then I watch her place the wand beneath the end of Mackenzie's gown.

"You are going to feel some pressure, but there shouldn't be any pain," the woman says.

Mackenzie's hand tightens around mine. "All right, relax for me," she instructs.

It takes a minute, but soon she finds whatever it is she's looking for—not that I can make anything out in the dark, grainy image on the screen.

"See here?" She points at the screen with the cursor. "That's your baby."

Squinting, I make out a head, but it mostly looks like a lima bean and nothing like a baby.

"Let's see if we can hear the heart." She flips a switch.

That's when my world is rocked. That's when it hits me. The sound of a swoosh, swoosh, swoosh fills the room. I drop my forehead to Mackenzie's and squeeze my eyes closed. "That's our baby," I say.

Mackenzie sobs. I want to gather her against me, but I know I can't. The sound is the most beautiful thing I have ever heard in my life.

"The heartbeat sounds great—it's really strong," the woman says.

I lift my head and look at the screen, at our child.

"I'm going to give the doctor the results of the ultrasound and let her go over them with you." She removes the wand and takes the condom off the end, tossing it and then her gloves in the garbage. She washes her hands. "Would you like me to print out a couple photos for you two to take with you?"

"Yes," we both say. She looks between the two of us and smiles. "Go on and get dressed. The doctor will be back in a few minutes to go over everything with you," she says as she leaves the room.

She hands me a few pictures before closing the door behind her.

Looking at the grainy image of our child, I ball my hand into a fist and try to control the worry that fills the pit of my stomach. Irrational worry. Tucking the picture away, I turn and help Mackenzie off the table, then take the paper gown from her and roll it into a ball and toss it into the trash as she starts to get dressed.

"I think we should move in together and get married."

"What?" She turns toward me and frowns as she starts to put on her dress.

"I think we should move in together and get married," I repeat, the idea making something inside of me feel more centered, more at ease.

"Did you hit your head?" She shakes hers before turning her back on me.

"No."

"Then you've lost your mind," she mutters. I step up behind her, wondering if I maybe have lost my mind. "We are not going to throw our already-crazy relationship into fast-forward just because I'm pregnant," she says.

I don't have a chance to tell her that I want to marry her because I'm in love with her. Because she is the best thing that has ever happened to me. Because I can't imagine things any other way. The second she finishes her statement, someone else knocks on the door.

"Come in," I growl, zipping up her dress.

She looks at me like I've lost my mind.

"Great news, guys." The doctor from earlier steps into the room. "Everything looks great. The baby's heartbeat is normal, and he or she seems to be developing well. So you're free to go. Just make sure you set up an appointment as soon as you can."

"I will, and thank you again," Mackenzie says, shaking her hand.

"Are you ready?" Mackenzie asks after the doctor leaves.

Part of me wants to force the issue of us getting married and living together, but seeing the exhaustion in her eyes, I know that now is not the time to harp on it.

"Yeah, gorgeous." I take her hand in mine. When we get out of the hospital, we have no choice but to catch a cab back to my place. I make sure that Mackenzie is buckled in on the ride home. Once we arrive at my place, we shower together and then get into bed and watch TV until we both fall asleep.

~

Hearing a song playing, I blink my eyes open. The room is completely dark, and Mac is tucked into my side with her hand resting on my abs. Hearing the song again, I sit up. I realize it's Mac's phone. Reaching over her to the bedside table, I pick it up and see in the light from the screen that she's opening her eyes. I lie back down.

"Who is it?" she asks sleepily.

"Your sister Fawn," I say.

She puts her hand to my gut and sits up, taking the phone from me and putting it to her ear.

"Hey, is everything okay?" she answers. "Oh my god! Shut up!" The tone of her voice changes from worried to excited in the blink of an eye, making me curious.

Sitting up, I reach over and turn on the light. Her happy, smiling eyes meet mine.

"I'm so happy for you—even if I am a little mad." She tucks the blanket under her arms. "Duh. Of course we will celebrate when you get home. All right. Love you, too. Tell Levi I said congrats, and give him a hug from me."

She hangs up.

"What's going on?"

"Fawn and Levi got married in Vegas tonight. I'm so happy for them."

"Me too," I agree, leaving out the part of me being a little jealous at the same time. Why didn't I think about taking her to Vegas?

"Fawn wants to have a small reception when they get home to celebrate." She grins before turning and dropping the phone on the side table.

"Do your parents know?"

"No." She shakes her head.

I wince, remembering Christmas dinner. "Your dad is going to be pissed."

"I know, but I think they did the right thing. If they had a normal wedding, Mom would have taken over the entire event, and Levi's mom would have been right there cheering Mom on. I think it's better that they got married in Vegas. Even if I'm a little annoyed that I didn't get to be there with her since that is something we've talked about since we were kids playing dress-up."

"We can go to Vegas and get married . . . ," I say.

She laughs like I'm joking, only I'm not joking at all. I'm being 100 percent serious.

"We're not getting married," she says, brushing me off and shaking her head with a smile on her face.

Lying back down in the bed, she closes her eyes. "I'm so tired." She yawns.

Sleep . . . seriously? Watching her breathing even out, I lie back down. But I don't sleep. I spend the rest of the night awake, wondering why the hell she doesn't want to marry me and what I can do to convince her that she does.

~

"Morning, sleepyhead." I greet Mackenzie with a kiss when she wanders out of the bedroom looking like she's still half-asleep. Her hair is a mess, and she has an indent on her cheek from the pillow. She's always beautiful to me, but there is nothing better than seeing her first thing in the morning wearing my T-shirt because she spent the night in my arms.

"Morning."

She squints her eyes at me, then at the coffeepot in my hand, which makes me smile.

Getting her a mug, I pour her a cup and hand it to her. I lean back against the counter and watch her wander around the kitchen, fixing the coffee to her liking.

"What's the plan for the day?" she asks once she's finished and taken her first sip from her cup.

"I have to work in a couple hours."

"Oh." She pouts before taking another sip of her coffee.

"Sorry, gorgeous."

"It's okay. Maybe I'll see if Libby wants to go see a movie with me."

She leans back against the counter across from where I'm standing. Her eyes heat as they slide up my abs and my chest.

I start to take a step toward her, but then I see her eyes stop on the bullet wounds on my shoulder. My whole body tenses because I know what's coming.

"You've never told me how you got those," she says quietly.

My hand tightens around the mug in my grasp.

"It was during a bust," I say. Then I ask, "What movie do you want to see?"

"Why don't you like talking about it?"

"Because I don't." I jerk a hand through my hair, and she flinches. "Sorry. Look, it's—"

"It's not a big deal." She cuts me off with a shrug, but I know that it is a big deal because I can see the hurt in her expression. "I should go."

She drops her still-full cup in the sink before she starts back toward the bedroom.

Grabbing her hand, I stop her before she can make it. Then I spin her around to face me. "I'm sorry. It was a long time ago, and I don't like talking about it."

"Why haven't you unpacked?" she asks, pointing at the boxes in the living room. I frown.

"What?"

"You still haven't unpacked. This place looks like it's not even lived in. There is nothing here that says an actual person lives here. A person with friends and family. A person who has a life and adventures. Why is that?"

"I don't know." I shrug, looking at the stack of boxes that holds my old life in them.

"You don't know, or you just don't want to tell me or talk to me about it?" she asks.

I see her chin wobble.

"I didn't say that, baby . . ." I soften my voice.

She shakes her head. "I know you didn't, but you also didn't have to. Anytime that I have touched that scar on your shoulder, you've closed down on me. Every time I've asked you what happened to you before you moved here, you've avoided answering. You tell me that you want to get married, but you won't even talk to me about things that are important. The things that have made you the person that you are today."

"None of that matters. All that matters is us. The person I am when I'm with *you*. The person that I am now."

"To you it doesn't matter, but to me it does." She pokes herself in the chest. "Whatever happened to you affects us. It affects you."

I jerk my hand thought my hair as my stomach clenches.

"My mom and dad are best friends. They talk about everything. They know everything about each other. The good *and* the bad stuff." Her jaw clenches. "I want that with the man I marry."

"I can't tell you about cases I'm working."

"I'm not asking you to tell me about cases that you are working, or even the cases that you have worked. I'm asking you to *talk* to me. I know that there is a story behind those scars you wear. And I'm not just talking about the scars that I can see, Wesley. I'm talking about the ones you keep hidden in there." She places her hand over my heart. "You say you want to marry me, but you don't even want to talk to me. You don't trust me with the things that are still hurting you."

"I trust you!" I roar.

She closes her eyes and takes a step back. That one step may as well be as big as the Grand Canyon between us. I know I should stop, that I should take this opportunity to open up to her about my past, but I can't. "Just drop it. None of that matters," I tell her.

She takes another step away from me. Like an accident happening in slow motion, I see her slipping further and further away.

"Never mind. You're not going to see things from my perspective. You are so determined to protect yourself that you're blind." She turns and heads for the bedroom.

"Where the fuck are you going?" I ask, following after her but stopping in the doorway.

"I need some time alone. I think you do, too," she whispers, putting on a pair of sweats from the bag that she brought over weeks ago. She grabs a sweatshirt out of the same bag and pulls it over her head before going to the corner of the room for her sneakers.

"You're running." I let out a humorless laugh.

She looks at me, shaking her head. I notice tears filling her eyes as she takes a seat on the side of the bed to put on her shoes.

"I'm *not* running," she finally says, lifting her head to look at me briefly.

"If you're not running, then what do you call it?"

"I call it giving us both time to think," she says quietly, dropping her gaze from mine.

"I call it being a coward," I snarl.

She flinches.

"When things get a little complicated or when you hear something you don't want to hear, you take off."

"That's not fair." She rubs her hands down her thighs as she stands. Then she wipes the tears from under her eyes.

I ignore the pang of regret that hits me. "I don't want to fight with you."

She picks up her bag from the floor and places it over her shoulder.

"Fuck this. Just go," I mutter, turning my back on her. I go into the bathroom and slam the door closed behind me. After turning on the water, I rest my hands on the basin and drop my head between my shoulders. I try to get my breath to even out. My heart feels about ready to pound out of my chest. Closing my eyes, I pull in a few deep breaths and let them out slowly. When I leave the bathroom a little while later, Mackenzie is gone.

She's taken my heart with her, just like I knew she would.

Chapter 12

BROKEN

MAC

Lifting my cell phone off my lap, I look at the screen when it starts to buzz. I close my eyes when I see that it's Wesley calling.

"Have you spoken to him yet?" Libby asks, taking a seat next to me on the couch.

I shake my head no as pain fills my chest.

"You really should talk to him."

She rests her head on my shoulder and places a hand over my stomach, which makes me want to cry. Then again, I have been doing a lot of crying this last week. A lot of crying, a lot of puking, and a whole lot of sleeping. Being pregnant is way more exhausting than I thought it would be. And it's not helping that things between Wesley and me are in such turmoil. We haven't spoken in a week.

Not since the moment he turned his back on me and left me standing in his room, crying.

He's called, left messages, and even stopped by more than once, but I can't talk to him or see him yet. I need a little more time. I need to make myself stronger before I face him. The minute I see him, I'm going to want to run right back into his arms and pretend like everything is okay when it's not. I didn't lie when I told him I didn't want to be with some-one who couldn't talk to me. And the idea of marrying him and living our life under the same roof while being psychological miles apart isn't appealing at all. I want a partner—someone to share the good and bad with—and it hurts that he doesn't see me as someone he can confide in.

Amazing chemistry alone isn't going to get us through this issue, that's for darn sure.

"I miss him," I say after a moment while rubbing the small baby bump that seemed to have popped up overnight. It's not huge or noticeable—unless I'm naked—but it is there. "I miss him, but I'm also really mad at him for not doing what I need him to do." I swallow down over the gravel lodged in my throat.

"Sometimes men are idiots," Libby says, sounding like she knows from experience. If I wasn't so caught up in my own personal drama, I would ask her about it because I know there is a story behind that statement. "He loves you."

"He might love me, but I want more than love. Maybe I'm being selfish, but I want all of him—not just the pieces that he's choosing to show me, not just the pieces of him that he can tie up in a neat little package for me."

"You're right. You deserve to have all of that—but so does he. He deserves to have someone to share his burdens with," she says.

Those stupid tears I've been trying to fight come back.

"Do you think I'm overreacting about this?" I ask after a few min-utes of listening to the television play in the background.

"Do *you*?"

"No . . . ? But I'm also pregnant and overly emotional right now, so I'm not sure I'm the best judge."

"Each woman has to decide for herself what she will and will not put up with in a relationship. If he won't talk to you about things that you can see are causing him pain, is that something you can deal with?"

"It isn't." I close my eyes and rest my cheek on the top of her head.

It isn't because I know that eventually, the pain he's carrying around is going to manifest itself in another way, and I won't watch him destroy himself—or put our child through seeing that firsthand, either. Pain has to be dealt with.

"When are you going to tell Mom and Dad about the baby?" she asks.

My muscles tighten and my stomach twists into a knot.

It doesn't feel right to tell anyone about the baby when things with Wesley and me are so up in the air. I don't want the announcement of being pregnant to be followed up with my telling everyone that Wesley and I won't be raising it together. The idea of doing that makes me feel even more sick.

"I don't know," I admit.

"You'll know when you're ready." She sits up. "I have to head to Tony's. Do you want me to bring you a slice of pizza home for dinner?" she asks.

My mouth waters at the offer, but not in a good way. Ugh. I can't even stand the thought of pizza now, and I love pizza—or I did. Yesterday, when Libby came home in the middle of the night smelling like it, I had to run for the bathroom.

"No, thank you." My face scrunches up.

"You haven't been eating much. Maybe you should ask your doctor about prescribing you something for the nausea."

"I'll call tomorrow," I agree.

She nods as she puts on her coat. "See you later."

"Later." I watch her shut the door, and then I lie down on the couch and feel sorry for myself while watching garbage TV. Eventually, I fall asleep.

WESLEY

After knocking, I take a step back and wait for someone to answer.

"Wesley! What are you doing here?" Katie asks, opening the door for me and then ushering me inside and out of the snowstorm that started about an hour ago.

Leaning down, I kiss her cheek. I'm half-surprised she doesn't smack me upside my head. I deserve to be smacked, and I also deserve to have my ass kicked.

"I stopped by to see Aiden. Is he around?" I follow her down a long hallway that's lined with photos of all three of the Reed girls.

"He's out back, in the shop." She stops at the glass double door in the kitchen and points to the backyard, across toward a large metal shed. "The snowblower is acting up, so he's trying to fix it before we get too much snow." She smiles. "Go on out, but make sure you stop back in before you leave. I made Mackenzie's favorite cookies—you can take her some," she says.

Pain rocks through me at the mention of her name, but so does a little bit of hope. Clearly, she still hasn't told her parents about our fight, which means she hasn't completely given up on me—or us—yet.

"Sure." I open the door, then head across the snow-covered lawn toward the shop. I can see Aiden inside, bent over a wooden workbench.

"Don't tell me you took my daughter to the courthouse and eloped," Aiden says by way of greeting when he spots me.

I smile for the first time in days.

"If you did, I suggest you turn and start to run, because I will shoot your sorry ass." He wipes his dirt- and oil-covered hands on a red towel before resting his hands on his hips.

"No, I didn't marry her. But when I'm done talking to you, I still may find myself needing to run," I say truthfully.

His brows pull together as he studies me with a fist on his hip and his feet spread wide. His size makes him an intimidating man, and so does his shaggy red beard. From his slightly defensive stance, I know I need to phrase what I'm about to say very carefully.

"What happened?" he asks, or rather growls.

Stepping into his shop, I take a seat in an old metal folding chair. I need to open up to someone, and I trust he'll understand.

I tell him everything. I tell him my reasons for moving to New York, about getting Mackenzie pregnant, and then finally I tell him about losing her because I'm a hardheaded idiot. When I'm done talking, he doesn't look happy, but I can tell that he doesn't hate me, either.

"You screwed yourself, didn't you?" he finally says.

I let out a long breath.

"Yeah." I swallow, leaning back and crossing my boot-covered feet and my arms over my chest. "I fucked up and lost the best thing that has ever happened to me."

It feels good to admit something that has been killing me since I forced Mackenzie to walk away from me.

"Is your heart still beating?" he asks.

I nod.

"Nothing is impossible unless you're dead. You're not dead, so you can still fix this."

"So how do I do that? How do I get her back?"

"I think the question you need to ask is how you fix *yourself*. You have to do that before you can fix what happened between you two. You've been torturing yourself because of what happened. You need to deal with that first, before you try and talk to Mac."

"You're right." I rub my hands against the stubble covering my jaw.

"Talk to someone about what happened. Be honest about how you feel, and then tell Mac. If I know my girl at all, I know she wanted to help you. You took that from her. Our girl may act like she's hard, but she's sensitive—she always has been," he says.

I know he's right, and that just adds to the guilt I've been feeling. I hate that I hurt her and that I didn't give her what she needed. I didn't open up to her, but that is all she was asking me to do.

"You're right."

"Now"—he leans back, crossing his arms over his chest—"let's talk about you getting my daughter pregnant without her having a ring on her finger."

"I—" I start to tell him that if I had my way, she would already have a ring on her finger, but he cuts me off.

"Save it. I don't expect you to marry her right now. Actually, I'd prefer if you didn't. What I want is for you to do right by her—and my grandchild."

"I always will!" I state vehemently. Family is the most important thing to me.

"Good," he says. His eyes and his voice both soften. "Now tell me—how is my grandbaby?"

"Healthy. I . . ." My lungs burn as I attempt to breathe through the sadness in my chest. I missed Mackenzie's doctor's appointment, but Libby sent me a text letting me know that everything was perfect. The doctors determined that Mackenzie was already about nine weeks along, so she must have gotten pregnant the day she came to get her phone.

"It will be okay." Aiden pats my shoulder, bringing me back from my thoughts. "You haven't lost her, so stop acting like you have. Women are crazy creatures. There are times you two are going to fight and think this is it, this is the end of us. Then the next day, you'll wake up with that dispute being nothing more than a memory. My daughter loves you, and I know you love her, so that right there will get you through everything."

"Thanks." I run my hand through my hair, then tuck my hands in the front pocket of my jeans. "I'm gonna head out before the roads get bad. They're predicting that the storm will dump eight to ten inches between tonight and tomorrow."

"I need to move to Florida." Aiden shakes his head.

I start for the door, smiling, but he stops me.

"Wesley?"

"Yeah?" I turn to look at him.

"If you need to talk, I'm here."

"Thanks." My throat clogs with emotion.

He lifts his chin by way of farewell, and I lift mine in return, then head out the door.

"Wesley!" He calls to my back again when I'm halfway across the yard.

I turn around once more. "Yeah?"

"You tell Levi when you see him that we are gonna have a few words next time I see him, so it might be best he keeps his distance for a bit."

"Will do."

I grin when I turn around and head back inside. I pick up the cookies from Katie for Mac before I get back in my truck and head home. Part of me wants to drive right over to Mackenzie's and tell her that I now understand what she was saying. That I get that she just wanted to help me. But I need to fight that urge until I take care of a few more things—even if it is killing me to stay away from her.

～

Cutting open the top of one of the packing boxes that I have ignored since I moved to New York, I take a breath. When you spend your whole life in one city and grow up with the same group of friends, good and bad memories tend to be connected to the objects you own. Dustin was part of most of the things I've kept locked away and unpacked so I wouldn't have to face the pain of losing him all over again. I didn't realize until I talked to a counselor who suggested I speak with his parents about that fact that I feel responsible for his death. The counselor said that talking with them might give me some closure, that hearing from them that they forgive me might set me on the road to healing.

So this afternoon, I called and talked to Dustin's mom and dad. They had told me before that what happened to Dustin wasn't my fault, but today was the first time I really heard them. I have been carrying around so much guilt, so much self-hate. From the beginning of our friendship, I was always Dustin's protector. He was the smaller, weaker one of the two of us, so it was my job to look out for him and to keep him safe. It had always been that way, from the day we met, when I stepped in and protected him from a couple of older kids who were picking on him. After that, we became best friends and were inseparable. I knew that he would always be in my life, and I would always be in his. We would probably name our kids after each other and force our wives to be best friends because we were. There would never be a time when we didn't have each other.

I close my eyes and remind myself that I can't go back or dwell on what could have been. Dustin wouldn't want that for me. If he knew the way I have been pushing everyone away since his death, he'd probably kick my ass. I know for sure he'd kick my ass if he knew about Mackenzie and the way I dismissed her feelings and her concern.

I pull out the first object in the box that my hands touch, and I smile when I see it's a photo of Dustin and me in our uniforms. We were twenty and had both just graduated from the academy. We thought we knew everything at that moment, but we learned quickly that we didn't know anything. Our first year on the force was the hardest and most fulfilling of them all. It taught us a lot about the men we were becoming. Setting the framed photo on the shelf, I spend the rest of the day unpacking box after box.

It's after eleven at night when I finally finish, but I can't sleep. All I can think about is tomorrow, when I plan on winning my woman back. I just pray that she accepts my apology. If she doesn't, I will just have to kidnap her and tie her to my bed.

Chapter 13

A Fresh Start

Mac

After the buzzer in my office goes off, I press the button to unlock the door and then pop a few more Tums in my mouth. On top of not sleeping and morning sickness, I have such bad heartburn that I have been eating Tums like candy.

"Knock, knock."

Seriously? I inwardly groan when Edward walks through my office door wearing a smile that makes me want to punch him in the face.

"What are you doing here?" I ask, trying to be polite. I'm honestly way too tired to play nice with anyone right now.

"Hello to you, too." He grins. "I thought I would stop by and see if you wanted to have lunch. I haven't seen or heard from you since New Year's."

"I've been a little busy." I sit back in my chair, praying the antacid works soon.

"Is everything okay?"

"Everything's fine," I lie. He studies me closely but doesn't say anything. He knows me well enough to pick up on the fact that I'm lying.

"Well, then, come on. Grab your coat, and let's go eat." I don't want to say yes, but then again I also don't want to spend the hour before my next client arrives sitting around feeling sorry for myself. I did that yesterday and the day before—and the day before that. The fact that Wesley hasn't called me in three days bothers me more than I want to admit. I mean, I wouldn't have answered if he *had* called, but he still *should* have called me. Then again, maybe the pregnancy is turning me into a crazy person.

"Are you coming?" Edward asks, snapping me back into the present.

"Fine." I grab my coat and my purse, and we head across the street to the deli. After ordering sandwiches, we take them to a table at the back and sit across from each other at a high-top table.

"How are things with you and Wesley?" he asks as we start to eat.

I finish chewing and swallow before I answer, "Okay." I'm intentionally vague because I don't want to start myself crying.

"Just okay? You two looked pretty in love on New Year's Eve. What happened since then?"

"We have both been busy. What's going on with you?"

"Work. The housing market has picked back up, so I'm busy most days."

"That's a good thing, right?"

"I need to pay for a wedding, so yeah—it's a good thing," he says.

My stomach twists.

"Can I ask you something?"

"Ask away." He takes an unconcerned drink from his soda and a bite from his sandwich.

"Why are you cheating on Bonnie?"

"I'm not."

"I heard you on the phone that day in my office. You were meeting another woman for sex—unless that was how Bonnie and you role-play. Or unless I misunderstood the whole conversation."

"It wasn't Bonnie," he says, balling up his napkin and tossing it into his empty sandwich basket.

"So you *were* talking to another woman?" I ask.

He nods.

"Why are you marrying Bonnie, then?"

"I love her."

"Do you?" I whisper, feeling sad for them.

"We have an open relationship," he says.

I blink at him. "Pardon?"

"Bonnie and I have an open relationship."

"Do you mean you guys are swingers?"

"Yeah." He runs his hand through his hair. "I love Bonnie, but I like other women, too. I just don't feel the same about them as I do her," he says.

I feel my lip curl up. I mean, to each their own, but there is no way I could live like that.

"Wow."

"That's why I never went there with you," he says.

I sit back in my chair. "What?"

"I knew you wanted to be more than friends, but let's be honest. You would never be okay with my lifestyle. So as much as I wanted to be with you, I knew I couldn't go there with you."

"Seriously?"

"I didn't want to risk losing our friendship," he says.

I shake my head. I can't believe I'm hearing any of this.

"I was going to send Bonnie an anonymous note to tell her you were an asshole and that you were cheating on her," I say.

He tosses his head back and laughs. "She would have gotten a kick out of that."

"I bet." I rub my hands over my face. I can't believe this. I guess I *can*, but still. "Well, this lunch has been enlightening," I say.

He smiles and stands up, and I do the same. Tossing my trash away, I walk him to the door, then back across the street to my office. I'm at a loss for words.

"Are we okay?" he asks, opening his arms to me.

I roll my eyes at him. "Yeah, we are okay."

"Good." He hugs me tighter before letting me go. "Also, if you and Wesley ever *do* decide that you want to try out a different lifestyle, let me know. Bonnie is a little crazy about your man, and I wouldn't mind—"

"Never going to fucking happen."

My heart drops into my stomach when the voice I love so much cracks through my office.

I spin around to face Wesley. Wesley, who looks a little scary and a whole lot handsome standing in my doorway.

"You will never, ever touch her." He glares at Edward before looking at me and softening his expression and tone. "Right, gorgeous?"

"Ugh . . ." I blink. "Right." I swallow.

"I figured that," Edward says.

I look at him just in time to catch the goofy smile he's wearing.

"I'll see you around. Maybe the four of us can do dinner sometime."

"*Probably* not," Wesley mutters at the same time I say, "Maybe."

I shrug, ignoring Wesley and his bristling. Edward kisses my cheek.

"We'll talk soon," he says. He looks at Wesley. "See you around, man."

"Hmm," Wesley grunts in response, watching Edward go.

Pulling my eyes from him, I wrap my arms around myself and take a few deep breaths before turning to look at him.

"What are you doing here?"

"I came to talk to you," he says, studying me from head to toe like he's memorizing every inch of me.

"About what?" I ask, not willing to get my hopes up.

"About everything."

"Everything?" I narrow my eyes, and he tucks his hands into the front pocket of his jeans. The move makes him look like a scared little kid.

"I messed up."

"I know," I agree.

There is no sense in coddling him—he *did* mess up. But then again, maybe we both messed up. He should have talked to me, and I shouldn't have run off because I was afraid.

Looking around my office, he shakes his head. "Are you busy now?"

"I have a client coming in soon, but it's my last one of the day."

"Will you come over to my place tonight so we can talk?" he asks.

I swallow over the lump forming in my throat.

"I don't know if your place is the best place for us to talk. We tend to end up in bed whenever we're there," I tell him quietly.

I see him clench his jaw.

"Right." He runs a hand roughly through his hair. "I'll meet you wherever you want to meet."

"There's a frozen-yogurt place across the street. How about we meet there in two hours?" I say.

Relief fills his eyes and his body relaxes.

"That's fine with me," he agrees, taking a step toward me.

My whole body goes on alert. I know the minute he touches me, I'm done for, so I can't let him touch me until we've talked and have gotten things sorted out.

"I miss you." The words sound pained, and it takes all my willpower not to go to him to soothe him—to soothe myself.

"Me too," I croak as my throat fills with tears.

"I'll see you soon, gorgeous."

"Sure." I watch him go. Closing my eyes, I pray that he's ready to open up to me. I don't know how much longer I can hold out.

WESLEY

As I wait on the sidewalk for Mackenzie to show up, my stomach fills with anxiety. The idea that she might not forgive me is something I can't handle. Seeing her come across the street toward me, I soak in everything about her. Her hair is up like it normally is when she's working; her face is clean of makeup, allowing her natural beauty to shine through; and she's wearing a long jacket that covers her from neck to knee so I can't see if her body has changed in the past week.

Jogging toward her, I meet her halfway across the street, then take her hand. "Hey."

She smiles up at me, and all I can think is, *God she's so beautiful, and I have missed her so much.*

With her hand in mine, we enter the frozen-yogurt shop. I wish it was farther away so I could keep my hold on her a little longer.

"Do you want to get some yogurt?" she asks me as she gets herself a big cup.

I shake my head. I just want to watch her. "I might have some of yours."

"No," she says bluntly as she pulls down the lever for chocolate. "I have been craving this for the last couple days. If you try to take any from my container, I might attack you," she says, making me smile.

"Are the cravings that bad?"

"This was the first time I've had one," she says softly.

Once again, I curse myself for having missed out on time with her.

"Have you had any other symptoms?" I ask, trying to remember what the book I got said happens in the first couple of months.

"I've had morning sickness, and heartburn so bad that I might have to buy stock in Tums," she says.

Every word makes me feel like shit. I should have been there to take care of her through this. Instead, I've been . . .

"Stop." Her hand presses into my chest, cutting off my wayward thoughts.

I drop my eyes to hers.

"Please stop."

Her words are soft, and I swear she knows where my mind is taking me.

"I'm sorry I wasn't there."

"Me too," she says quietly, finishing up her serving and heading toward the cashier. I pull out my card to pay—noticing that the frozen yogurt is overflowing the container—then lead her to the back of the store, where there is no one around.

"What did you want to talk to me about?" she asks.

I can see the doubt in her eyes. I can tell she doesn't think I will open up to her.

"My best friend from childhood was also my partner back in Seattle," I tell her.

The spoon in her hand pauses an inch from her mouth.

"We had so many plans for the future. Then, one day, that was all taken from me."

"What happened?" she asks.

I close my eyes, remembering the day like it was yesterday.

"We were on a routine drug bust. After we got into the house and had already made our arrest, we started collecting evidence. Suddenly, gunshots started going off. We all dropped, not knowing that we were setting ourselves up for disaster. None of my team realized that the shots were being fired from a man hiding in the attic—until it was too late. I took three bullets to the shoulder, but not before seeing Dustin take a bullet to the head. He died right in front of me," I say.

Tears fill her eyes.

"I blamed myself for his death. I had always protected him, but I didn't protect him when it really mattered."

"It wasn't your fault." She wipes her eyes.

"I know." I gasp in anticipation as she stands up from her chair.

She slides into my lap—where she belongs, and where she will always belong.

"I should have opened up to you, gorgeous. You were right. I should have talked to you. I should have trusted you with everything. I was afraid you would think I was weak and a coward because that's what I have been telling myself I am for so long."

"You're the strongest guy I know. You could never be weak." She rests her lips against mine. "I'm so sorry for leaving. I shouldn't have left."

"I'm not." I kiss her because I can, because I've missed being able to kiss her when I want. "I wouldn't have dealt with my issues if you hadn't left. I would have continued to ignore it all, like I had been doing." I push her hair back out of her face. "Because of you, I finally got the closure I needed. And I finally heard what Dustin's parents have been trying to tell me for a long time."

"I'm glad you got that," she says, running her fingers up my jaw and into my hair. "I love you. You know that, right?" she asks.

I press my forehead to hers, wondering how the hell I came to deserve her.

"I know. I don't know *why* the fuck you love me, but I'm glad you do."

"I love you because you love *me* just the way I am. I love you because you make me feel special, because you make me laugh, you make my soul happy . . . and because you give me really great orgasms."

She says the last bit quietly, and I smile.

"I do, don't I?" I say smugly.

She laughs. "Yeah, you do." She shifts her fingers through my hair once again, studying me.

"Are we okay?"

"Yes." She kisses my cheek. "Now let me finish my yogurt."

She gets off my lap and takes a seat across from me.

"What was that whole thing with Edward about?" I ask.

She drops her spoon and covers her face, cracking up. Eventually she pulls herself together enough to tell me. When she does, I'm the one who can't stop laughing.

~

"Oh my god. Hurry." Mackenzie jumps up and down at my side as I put the key in the lock.

"It's hard to focus when your tits are bouncing around like that," I say. She smacks my chest and laughs. "There you go."

I open the door, and she runs into my apartment ahead of me, straight for the bathroom. Shutting the door, I drop my keys and the pizza on the table. I take off my jacket and hang it on the back of a chair.

When she comes out of the bathroom, she freezes in place and then swings her head around the living room.

"You unpacked."

"I did."

She does a circuit around the living room, looking at the photos and all the stuff that is now out and on display.

"You two looked like you were troublemakers," she whispers, stopping in front of one of the pictures of Dustin and me. In the photo, we're playing cards with a few other guys—unbeknownst to them, the two of us were cheating everyone else at the table and winning.

"We *were* trouble." I laugh.

"I think I would have liked him. He had kind eyes," she says.

My eyes burn with unshed tears.

"You would have liked him, but he would have liked you more. He loved women—all women," I say. She laughs, turning to look at me over her shoulder.

"Thank you for sharing him with me."

Her words hit me in the chest and gut at the same time, making it almost impossible to breathe. I should have told her about him a long time ago. I should have known that she would help me heal. If anyone could, I should have known it would be her.

"You're welcome, gorgeous." I take her hand and pull her toward me. "I went and talked to your dad."

"You went and talked to my dad?" she repeats, looking nervous. "Why?"

"Because I respect him. Because I wanted his opinion on what to do about you."

"Okay. Was everything okay? What did he tell you?" she asks, biting her bottom lip.

"It was fine." I tuck a piece of hair behind her ear. "He told me to trust you."

"To *trust* me?" She frowns, looking confused.

"He told me to trust you to heal me. I should have known that you would do that without having to have him tell me," I say.

Her eyes soften, then narrow.

"What are you *not* telling me about your meeting?"

"I told him that you are pregnant," I admit.

Her eyes get wide. "*You* told my dad I was pregnant?" she whispers, looking stunned.

"I did."

"Oh my god." She hits my chest with the palms of her hands. "My mom is going to *freak out* that I didn't tell her."

"It will be okay," I say. She raises a brow, and I shrug. "Maybe he hasn't told her yet."

"Maybe." She nibbles her bottom lip, then looks at the clock. It's already after nine.

After we left the yogurt shop, we made a couple of stops before we came back to my place. We stopped to get her some clothes, then we stopped at Tony's so that she could tell Libby she was staying with me. When we got to the pizza parlor, we found Libby behind the counter, taking orders from customers and bossing a group of men around in the kitchen. Not that any of them noticed that they were being bossed around by her—they all seemed to love the attention. This seemed to annoy the shit out of Antonio, who was mostly glowering in Libby's direction.

"Maybe you're right. Maybe he didn't tell her," she says, bringing me out of my thoughts.

I gather her close.

"He probably didn't tell her. I think she would have called when she found out."

I slide my hand up the back of her shirt, then around to her stomach. Feeling a small bump there, I take a step back and lift up her top to get a better look.

"When did this happen?"

"Two days ago. I woke up, and it was like that," she says.

I lead her into the bedroom and take off her shirt before I lay her down on the bed to get a better look. To see if I'm imagining things.

"Holy shit," I mutter, getting onto the bed.

She moves my hand so it's resting on our growing child.

"I know." She runs her fingers through my hair.

I look up at her, then place a kiss on her stomach. Her eyes get dark.

"Wesley."

"Yeah?" I pull her pants down over her hips, then toss them to the floor behind me. This leaves her in a sheer bra and matching panties that barely cover anything. Removing her panties, I toss them to the floor and then open her legs. Sliding my fingers between the lips of her pussy, I place my mouth against hers as my fingers begin to slowly circle her clit. I slide them down over her entrance, and her hips begin to move with my hand. She's so wet that my fingers slide over her with no resistance. "Did you miss me?" I slide two fingers deep inside her.

"Yes," she whimpers. I begin to move my fingers faster, and her pussy gets tighter. I know she is going to come, but I miss her taste so I pull my fingers out of her.

"I'll give them back to you in a second," I say when she looks at me as I get off the bed and get undressed.

Her eyes lock on my cock, and I swear it grows under her gaze. "Do you want this?" I wrap my fist around it, pumping two times.

"Yes," she whimpers again as I climb back on the bed and move between her legs.

After kissing her mouth, I move my way down her body. I kiss each of her nipples, licking, sucking, and biting them. The noises she's making and her nails digging into my hair egg me on once I have given both breasts the same treatment. I kiss down her stomach, licking around her belly button before lowering myself and lifting one of her legs up and over my shoulder. I sit back so I can watch my fingers enter her in smooth strokes, then start fucking her harder with two fingers before lowering my face and licking right up her center, pulling her clit into my mouth.

The heel of her foot digs into my shoulder, and her pussy clamps down on my fingers right before her body goes completely limp. Kissing her clit one last time, I wipe my chin on her inner thigh. I kiss my way up her stomach and slide into her, resting my forehead against her collarbone as her pussy spasms.

"I've missed you so much." She wraps her limbs around me, holding me close.

I drop my forehead to hers.

"Fuck, gorgeous, I've missed you, too. You feel so good," I tell her, raising my head above hers. "So fucking good."

I move slowly, our bodies sliding against each other easily. Her legs lift and wrap tight around my ass, pulling me deeper. So deep that I bump her cervix.

"Oh god," she cries as her nails dig into my back.

"I feel it, gorgeous. Fuck, you are squeezing me so tight. Fuck!" I growl, planting myself balls-deep inside her as her orgasm pulls me over the edge. She sucks every last drop of cum from me. Rolling to my back with her in my arms and my cock still buried inside her, I pull the covers up from the bottom of the bed and toss them over us.

Listening to her breathing even out while my hand runs over her hair, I eventually follow her off to sleep.

MAC

A pounding noise coming from somewhere wakes me. I squint one eye open, then the other. "What is that?" I ask Wesley.

He sits up, turning on the side lamp and casting the room in soft light.

"Someone is at the front door." He gets out of bed and puts on a pair of sweats, looking ready to murder whoever it is.

"What time is it?" I ask, unable to see the clock from my side of the bed.

"Six thirty." He picks up a baseball bat from beside the bed on his way out of the room.

"Six thirty?" I repeat, shaking my head.

"You got my daughter pregnant!"

I shoot out of bed when I hear my mom's voice shrieking.

"I can't believe you didn't tell me about this! I can't believe I had to find out from Mackenzie's father that you two are expecting my first grandchild!" she continues loudly as I stumble around.

Rummaging across the floor, I search for something to wear. Finding a pair of Wesley's sweats and one of his long-sleeve shirts, I put both on quickly, then rush out into the living room.

Mom is standing there, looking like a madwoman. She has curlers in her hair, oversize glasses on the end of her nose, and she's wearing a pink, fluffy bathrobe that has seen better days—those days being when my sisters and I bought it for her, when we were little.

"Mom, what the hell?" I blurt.

She looks at me. "You didn't *think to tell me* that you're pregnant with my grandchild?" She crosses her arms over her chest and hitches out one hip. She starts tapping her foot.

"We were waiting to tell everyone," I say, feeling like I did when I was a kid and she would get mad at me for misbehaving.

"Wesley told your dad." She points accusingly at Wesley, who is standing shirtless in the kitchen drinking a glass of water like he doesn't have a care in the world, like this situation is normal and happens every day. "That is *not* you waiting to tell everyone."

"I know." I look at Wesley and narrow my eyes at him.

He shrugs as if to say, "What am I supposed to do?"

"This is all your fault," I mouth.

He smiles back, mouthing, "Love you."

"Where is Dad?" I ask Mom. I honestly expected him to follow her dramatic burst into the apartment.

"He's in the car. He didn't want to search for parking or double-park in case a cop drives by." She waves off my question.

"You could have called. You didn't have to come all the way into the city."

I sigh and run a hand through my hair. Not that her coming into the city surprises me. I knew as soon as Wesley told me that he told my dad that it wouldn't be long before my mom found out. I should have called her last night and told her the news myself. We could have avoided all this drama.

"And have you avoid my call? No way." She shakes her head. "You and your sisters are going to be the death of me. First Fawn runs off and gets married on New Year's in Vegas just to avoid planning a wedding. And now you don't tell me that you're pregnant, but your boyfriend tells your dad. And then Libby . . ."

"Libby?" I say, wondering what the hell Libby could have done.

"Yes, Libby bought a pizza restaurant. Did she tell me about it?" she asks, then shakes her head. "No, she told your dad and had him help her get the loan."

I blink.

"Did you just say that Libby bought a pizza place?"

"I did."

"Oh my god. She didn't tell me," I whisper. I knew that she had been working at Tony's a lot lately, but I had no idea she was going to *buy* it. She never even mentioned it being for sale.

"Well, how does it feel?" Mom asks like a little kid saying *neener, neener, neener.*

I shake my head at her. It doesn't feel good, but it's not the same thing. Libby is my sister, not my mom. Then again, Libby did tell me that she was going to stop sharing things in her life because Fawn and I had been closed off about what was going on in *our* lives. We kinda deserved this, but that doesn't change the fact that I will kick her ass for not telling me.

"Mom . . . ," I say.

She looks at me.

"Wesley and I are pregnant. Right now, your grandchild is about nine weeks old and doing awesome," I say.

She covers her mouth, and tears fill her eyes.

"Oh, Mom." I go to her and wrap my arms around her shoulders. "I'm sorry I didn't tell you. I didn't plan on telling anyone yet. They say you should wait until you are twelve weeks along," I say.

Wesley makes a noise, so I look at him. "What?"

"Nothing."

I know he's lying—I can tell by the look in his eyes.

"What did you do?" I ask in a huff.

"I told my mom and Levi," he admits, looking sheepish.

"What?" I can't believe that he's already been telling people.

"I didn't know that we were supposed to wait until twelve weeks. In my defense, you never told me that," he says. I close my eyes and lean my head back to look at the ceiling.

"You know what? Whatever. It doesn't matter." I rest my head on my mom's shoulder and ask, "Are you happy, Mom?"

Forcing me away from her, she looks me in my eyes. "All I have ever wanted for you girls is happiness. Seeing you each get that in your own ways makes me more than happy," she says softly.

Now it's time for my eyes to fill with tears.

"I'm so happy for you. I'm so happy that you found your own happiness."

"Thank you, Mom." I wipe my eyes. "I love you."

"I love you, too, honey." She kisses her fingers and places them against my lips.

"Even though you are crazy, you are the best mom a girl could ever ask for." I pull her in for one more hug before letting her go. "Now go home before traffic backs up and people going to work are stuck looking at your crazy morning getup."

"I was in a rush to get here." She pats her head, and I laugh.

"I can tell," I say.

She smacks my shoulder. "Love you," she murmurs. She looks at Wesley. "Come give me a hug," she commands him.

He comes across the room and wraps her in his arms. She gives a thumbs-up in my direction. Hugging Wesley shirtless is definitely worth a thumbs-up, so I get it. "All right." She looks between us after she lets him go. "I expect you two over for breakfast or dinner when you both have a day off."

"We'll set up a time soon." I open the door for her. "Tell Dad I love him."

She waves over her shoulder as she heads up the stairs. Watching her go, I shake my head. I'm sure a few people saw her on the sidewalk this morning, and I have no doubt that they all thought she was a crazy person.

"I like your mom," Wesley says, wrapping his arms around me and leading me back into the bedroom.

"Do you?" I ask as he pulls his shirt off over my head.

"I do."

He strips off my pants and his own, then helps me into the bed.

"Did you tell anyone else about the baby?" I ask.

His finger on my hip stops moving.

"I did," he says.

I wait for a list of names, but he doesn't continue.

"Who else did you tell?"

"Just a few guys from work." He kisses the top of my head before settling me impossibly closer.

"You're happy," I whisper, realizing that he keeps telling everyone because he's excited about becoming a dad.

"I'm so happy." He tips my head back with two fingers under my chin so he can kiss me once more.

"I'm happy you're happy."

Kissing his pecs, I close my eyes and say a silent thank-you to whoever it is watching over us and our happily ever after.

Epilogue

MAC

"No." I pull another pair of shorts out of my drawer and toss them behind me. "No, no, no." I toss item after item behind me and let out a frustrated breath. None of my stuff fits anymore. In the last seven and a half months, I have gained just about fifty pounds, most of it in the last few weeks. Holding my hands against my naked stomach, I look down at my huge bump.

"Kid, you're lucky I love you." My stomach moves like our son knows what I'm saying, and I laugh. I don't know if I will ever get used to him moving around—it's the weirdest and most magical feeling I have ever experienced in my life.

"Are you about ready?" Wesley asks. I lift my head just as he walks into the bedroom. "I guess not."

He smiles, his eyes raking over my breasts and stomach.

"I can't find anything to wear."

"What about those shorts you wore the other day?"

I look at the pile behind me, then back at him.

"I can't. They don't fit anymore. Nothing fits me anymore." I take a seat on the side of the bed, completely drained from trying on clothes for the last thirty minutes. "My bras don't even fit." I lie back and rest my hands over my full, achy breasts.

"Do you want to go shopping?"

"When have I *ever* wanted to go shopping?" I ask.

He laughs as he lies down next to me. Taking my hand, he lifts it to his mouth and kisses my fingers, making my stomach melt.

"We could just stay home," he suggests, sucking my ring finger into his mouth.

I laugh and tug my hand from his grasp.

"We can't miss the Fourth of July at my parents' house. I'll just go see if I can't find a dress or something," I say. I yawn, covering my mouth.

His eyes fill with concern.

"I'll go get you something to wear."

"*You'll* go?" I repeat.

He shrugs, turning to his side to face me. "Yeah, I'll go. That way you can take a nap. I know you were up most of the night."

"That's because your son sleeps most of the day and is up all night using my bladder as a soccer goal."

"I know." He wraps his hand around my stomach. "I keep telling him to let you rest, but he doesn't seem to be listening."

"He's stubborn," I agree, placing my hand over his on my stomach.

"I wonder where he gets that from." He smiles, and I narrow my eyes on his.

"Shouldn't you be on your way?" I snap.

Chuckling, he kisses my nose. "Do you have any requests?"

"Requests?"

"Do you know what you would like me to get for you?"

"Something big." I look down at my stomach and revise. "Really big."

"You're not big, gorgeous. You're pregnant with our son."

"Yeah, your son who is already nine pounds." I remind him of the news the doctor delivered two days ago at our last appointment. "Our boy is now the size of a bowling ball, and we still have about five weeks until his due date."

"His dad is a big guy." He winks, and I roll my eyes.

"So arrogant."

"You love me."

"Yeah," I agree softly as he glides his fingers across my forehead and down behind my ear. "How did I get so lucky?"

"I ask myself that same question every day." He rolls me to my back and looms over me. Looking up into his love-filled eyes, I feel tears sting my nose. I don't know that I will ever get used to him loving me the way he does. So completely. "Don't cry." He laughs, wiping away the tears.

I cover my face. Since becoming pregnant, I cry all the time about the dumbest stuff, which is so annoying.

"I'm not crying," I sniffle.

I hear him laugh.

"I'm not . . . ," I gripe.

"Good." He pulls my hands from my face, kisses me once more, then sits back. "Let me go so I can get back here."

"I'm not holding you hostage." I sit up and scoot back to rest against the headboard.

"You're mostly naked."

"And?"

"And it's distracting." He circles my nipple with his thumb, and my eyes slide closed. "Gorgeous, I need to leave."

My eyes fly open, and I find him smiling at me. "So go, then." I cover my chest, and he laughs.

"Do you love me?"

"No," I tease.

His grin widens.

"Whatever." I push at his chest. "Hurry and come back."

"I won't take long." He kisses my forehead, then my lips before he pushes up out of bed.

Watching him as he leaves the room, I smile. Then I reach down, pull a quilt up over myself, and lie down.

~

"Hey, gorgeous." I blink my eyes open and find Wesley sitting on the side of the bed. "I've been trying to wake you up for about ten minutes now," he says, studying me.

I sit up, then scoot back in the bed. "Really?" I rub my eyes.

"You're tired." He rests his hand on my stomach. "Are you sure you want to go out to your parents' house?"

"I'm sure. Besides, I can sleep in the car on the way there, or take a nap there if I need to," I say.

I can see in his eyes that he doesn't like the idea.

Tipping my head to the side, I rest my hand over his. "I'm okay."

"I know you're exhausted."

"I know, but that's because I've been growing a human," I joke, but Wesley doesn't laugh.

He takes his job of taking care of me very seriously. Getting up on my knees, I wrap my arms around his neck and kiss his cheek.

"I'm fine," I say.

He turns to look at me, then slides his hand up my back and into my hair. Pulling my mouth down to his, he touches his lips to mine.

"Promise me that if you need to rest, you will rest."

"I promise." I give him a salute. "Now let's see what you got for me."

I hold out my hand, and he picks up the bag and passes it to me. Opening it up, I fight back a laugh as I pull out the dress to get a better look at it.

"Well, it's definitely festive." I stand up and hold the red, white, and blue dress up in front of me. The top of the dress is dark blue with white stars, and the bottom part is red and white stripes.

"There weren't a lot of options," he says, sounding unsure. "Is it okay?"

"It's perfect."

I go to him, wedge myself between his spread thighs, and his hands move to my stomach. He drops his forehead and rests it there.

"Thank you."

I run my fingers through his hair, and he tips his head back to look at me. I bend at the waist as best I can and touch my mouth to his, then take a step back and put on my new dress over my head. The band that wraps around my breasts is a little snug, but besides that, the rest of the material skims over my stomach and slides down my body. It just touches the floor. Going across the room, I check myself out in the mirror, turning side to side. I look very patriotic.

"You look beautiful."

"Thank you." I meet his gaze in the mirror and shake my head when I see how dark his eyes are. He is really in love with my pregnant body. I don't get it, but I do appreciate that he still finds me attractive. "Are you ready?"

"As ready as I'm going to be." He stands up from the bed and comes up behind me, wrapping his arms around me, settling his hands on my waist, and his chin on the top of my head. "Remember what you promised?"

"I remember . . ." I roll my eyes, then turn in his arms and get up on tiptoes and peck his lips. "Let me finish getting ready, and we can go."

"Take your time." He kisses my forehead, then turns me toward the door. Going past the living room, I head into the bathroom and finish getting ready. I hear the TV turn on. I have no doubt that he's watching one of his guy shows while working on either the crib or the dresser we picked up from Ikea a few days ago. Both things came in a million pieces. I didn't even pretend to know where to start, which left him on his own.

After brushing out my hair, I put it up in a bun, then put on some tinted moisturizer, blush, and mascara. Once I'm done, I head into the kitchen and pull out my ever-present pitcher of grape Crystal Light. I'm so addicted to the stuff that I drink about a quart a day. After filling up my tumbler, I take it with me to the living room and take a seat on the couch to watch Wesley finish one more dresser drawer.

"Do you think we should move?" I ask.

He stops what he's doing.

"I know we said we would wait until after he gets here, but we only have the one bedroom, and he seems to be accumulating a lot of stuff already," I say, looking around the living room.

Last month, my sisters threw me a baby shower, and we got so many diapers and other things that we will need for the baby that there isn't any room left in the apartment for us.

"Gorgeous, you are in no shape to move. I'm not going to put you through that right now. We'll move after the baby's born."

"Don't you think it will be harder to move with a newborn?" I ask.

He looks around, then down at my stomach. He drops his face into his hands for a moment and grumbles something I can't make out.

"We need to go to your parents'." He stands and pulls me up to stand with him.

Grabbing his hand, I stop him before he can get away. "What's going on?"

"Nothing. We just need to hit the road if we're going to make it there in time for lunch."

"Are you sure?"

"I'm sure." He bends and kisses me quickly before leaning back. "Let's go."

I grab my bag from the top of the kitchen table and then take his hand and follow him out of the house. The car is parked a block away. Once there, he helps me in, then jogs around to get behind the wheel. Checking my cell phone, I see a text from Fawn letting me know that she and Levi just arrived out on Long Island and that traffic was horrible.

"Fawn said they just got to Mom and Dad's, and that traffic is backed up."

"It's all right. We'll make it there in time for the fireworks," he says.

I laugh while turning to put on my seat belt.

"Oh." I pull in a quick breath as a sharp pain shoots through my abdomen.

"Are you okay?"

"I think so."

"You *think* so?" he repeats, sounding on edge.

"I . . . Oh!" I grab hold of my stomach when another sharp pain hits me.

"You're not okay," he growls.

I bite my lip. He's right, I'm *not* okay.

"I'm taking you to the hospital."

"It's too soon for me to have the baby."

"It's not too soon." He rests his open palm over my stomach. "He's already nine pounds, and his lungs are developed. If he's coming early, everything will be okay. Okay?"

"Okay." Feeling slightly reassured, I take one deep breath, then another, as he pulls the car out into traffic and rushes us to the hospital. We call my parents and everyone on the way.

WESLEY

"Push!" the doctor instructs.

Mackenzie bears down once more while squeezing my fingers so tight that I swear she's going to cause them to fall off from lack of blood flow.

"You're doing so good, gorgeous. Just keep pushing," I encourage gently.

"Shut up! No one wants your stupid advice! It's your fault that I'm in this situation, you jerk!" she screams, her face turning red.

I would be offended by the outburst, but just minutes ago she was telling me how much she loved me. Since going into labor, she has adopted multiple personalities.

"I know it's my fault. I'm sorry," I agree. She squeezes harder.

I hate this. I hate that she's in pain.

"Okay, relax for me," the doctor says.

She falls back on the bed and closes her eyes. Taking the wet washcloth off her brow, I kiss her forehead and replace it with a new one that's cold.

"I see the head. Let's go again!" the doctor calls.

I hold on to her hand and pull back her knee while the nurse across from me does the same thing.

"He's here!" the doctor says.

I stupidly look down between Mackenzie's legs, instantly regretting it when I see blood—lots of blood—and a round object ripping her open.

"He's going down!" I hear someone shout at the other end of the tunnel I've fallen into, right before everything goes dark.

Hearing a beep, beep, beep, I squint my eyes open against the bright light above me. Someone is shining a flashlight in my eyes.

"Welcome back." Mackenzie smiles at me, and I shake my head and sit up.

"What happened?"

"You passed out," the nurse says while she rolls her eyes.

"I passed out . . ."

I look around, and my stomach drops. Seeing Mackenzie adjust a bundle of blankets against her chest, everything comes back to me. Baby! She was having our baby. Quickly getting up, I rush across the room and straight through the nurses moving around at her side.

"Are you okay? Are you both okay?"

"We are both fine." She pulls back the edge of the blanket, and tears fill my eyes as I fall instantly in love for the second time in my life.

Our son is adorable. He's the perfect mixture of his mom and me. When he opens his eyes and looks up at me, the tears I was trying to control spill over.

"I know that we were still trying to come up with a name for him," she says.

I kiss the top of his head.

"Do you have an idea?" I ask, sliding my fingers across his fuzz-covered head.

"Dustin."

"Really?" My voice sounds like I just swallowed gravel.

"He looks like a Dustin, doesn't he?" she asks, touching her fingers to his nose and then his chin.

"He does," I agree, resting my lips on her forehead. "Thank you, gorgeous."

"For what?" She pulls her eyes from our boy to look at me.

"For everything. For bringing me back to life and giving me something to fight for."

"I love you, Wesley." She tucks her forehead into my throat, and I hold her and our son. I vow then and there to keep them safe always.

Seven months later . . .

WESLEY

"I love you, gorgeous, but if your mom doesn't give me my boy and get the hell out of our house, I'm going to lose my mind," I growl, standing above Mackenzie in the bathtub. Seeing her naked is making me hard, but I try to ignore that.

Peeking up at me, she squints her eyes. "You want me to go out and tell my mom to hand over her grandson and go home?" she asks, sounding like my request is irrational.

"Yes." I cross my arms over my chest.

She stands up in the bath, and water skims down her body. God, I thought I couldn't keep my hands off her before the pregnancy, but since she's had our son, I have become obsessed—or more obsessed—than ever.

"Do not even think about it." She holds out her hand, pressing it against my chest when I take a step toward her. "Please hand me a towel." She wiggles her fingers.

Reluctantly, I hand one over and watch her cover herself up. Without even bothering to dry off, she stomps past me, through the bedroom, and into the living room. She comes to a stop in front of her mom, who is sitting on the couch cooing at seven-month-old Dustin.

"Mom, what did I tell you about giving Dustin to Wesley when he asks for him?" she asks, crossing her arms over her towel-covered chest.

"I was feeding him," Katie lies, trying to look innocent.

Everyone knows that the woman is a baby hog.

"Well, he's not eating now. So please hand him over to his father so that he can spend some time with him and I can continue taking my bath."

"Oh, fine," she huffs as she stands. Bringing him to me, she mutters "snitch" under her breath. She gives me the evil eye before kissing my son and placing him in my arms.

She heads off to the front door, where she picks up her purse. "I won't see you guys until next weekend."

"Bummer . . . ," I mutter only loud enough for Mackenzie to hear.

She smacks my chest before walking toward her mom.

"Thank you for coming over and watching Dustin for us today."

"Anytime." She gives Mackenzie a peck on the cheek and me another glare before she leaves.

I ignore the look—I'm used to them. She and I constantly go round and round about Dustin. On the one hand, I love that she's always willing to step in when we need her. On the other, when I want my son, I want my son. I probably shouldn't have bought a house down the block from Mackenzie's parents. I didn't think about what it would be like to live so close to her mom.

"Thank you, gorgeous." I kiss the side of Mackenzie's head when her mom leaves.

She rolls her eyes, then heads back to the bathroom. I take Dustin into the bedroom. Lying down with him on the bed, I stare into his eyes. They look just like his mom's. I smile when he does.

"I know you like spending time with your grandma, but she has to learn to share," I tell him.

He smiles a toothless smile, then babbles something I can't make out. Probably something about how much he loves his grandma.

"I know, kid," I agree, bringing him to my chest and holding him there. I close my eyes and listen to my son's breath even out, then I fall asleep with him.

When Mackenzie gets out of the bath, she wakes up both of us.

"One more," I say to Mackenzie as she tucks Dustin into his bed, bending over the side to kiss his forehead.

"I don't know." She shakes her head, running her finger down our son's cheek.

She hasn't gotten on birth control since Dustin was born, and I have been attempting to convince her for weeks that we should have another baby. She wants to wait until after we get married. I told her that it doesn't matter. We can get married at the courthouse as soon as she wants—the only rule is that her dad gets to be there to give her away.

"Who knows how long it will take to conceive? We got lucky last time, and that is not always the case . . . ," I remind her as we get into bed. Curling to my side, I wrap my hand around her hip. "I want Dustin to have a sibling to grow up with. I want him to have a best friend."

"Wesley . . . ," her husky voice calls.

I dip my chin to find her head tipped back and her sleepy eyes on me. Taking her in, all I can think is how beautiful she is.

"Yeah?" I ask.

She touches my chin as I run my finger across her hairline and tuck her hair behind her ear, watching her pupils dilate as her hips shift against mine. Without answering, she slides her body up and wraps her hand around my jaw.

"Okay," she whispers.

"Okay, what?"

"Okay, let's have another baby," she answers against my lips.

A growl vibrates in my chest, and I lean forward while sliding my fingers through her hair at the side of her head. I pull her mouth closer to mine, and her lips part without command, allowing my tongue to touch hers. The moment her taste hits me, I know I won't be able to slow down or stop. Like always, my need for her is more than I can control. Pulling her up to straddle my waist, I sit up, then cup her ass and slide inside her. Connecting with her like this centers me. There is nothing better than being inside her. Using my hands on her hips, I control her movements and slow her down. "Like this." I rock her hips, and her head falls back. Her cascading hair hits the tops of my thighs. Listening to her moan, I slide my hands up her waist and cup her breasts, pulling her nipples. Her body bucks, and her forehead drops to my chest.

"Wesley . . ."

"Give me your mouth," I growl.

She lifts her head and looks at me through lust-filled eyes. Sitting up, she leans forward and covers my mouth with hers. I lick into her mouth and listen to her whimper as I lift my hips up into hers.

"I'm so close."

"I know, gorgeous." I feel her walls clamp down around me; then she moves her hand between our bodies. I know what she's reaching for. "Lean back. I want to watch you touch yourself." I help her sit back, then watch as she works her clit while riding me. "Christ, do you know how beautiful you look filled with my cock?" I pull her nipples, and she moans even louder while her pussy convulses, making my balls tighten up and my spine tingle. Knowing I'm getting close, that I'm about to lose it, I sit up and capture one breast. I suck her nipple hard while pulling and tugging the other. "Fuck! Ride me harder," I growl.

She starts to rock against me with more force than before. I listen to her whimper right before she starts to come, her pussy strangling my cock. Lifting my hips up into hers, I come deep inside her and groan my release around her nipple.

Her body slumps against mine, and I wrap my arms around her and tuck my face into her neck.

"I love you," she whispers when our breathing has evened out.

I squeeze my eyes closed. I will never get used to hearing those words from her. Never.

Ten months later . . .

MAC

Staring up at the ceiling, watching the morning light move across the surface, I smile. Wesley wraps his hand around my waist on one side of me, and Dustin tosses his tiny arm over my neck on the other. Dustin doesn't normally sleep with us, but I think that he is still so wired after Christmas yesterday that he couldn't sleep—meaning he woke up and there was nothing we could do to get him back to sleep in his own bed. Eventually we both gave up trying and just let him sleep in here with us. He started out between his dad and me, but at some point he must have moved to my other side. So I'm now sandwiched between my boys. Feeling the need to use the restroom, I carefully scoot out from between them and get off at the end of the bed.

After grabbing Wesley's flannel robe on the way to the bathroom, I put it on and wrap it around my waist. Stepping over unwrapped toys and stacks of clothes that still need to be put away, I go into the bathroom and bite my lip when I see the pregnancy test I set on the counter last night.

Opening the box, I scan the directions and then take the test. I set it on the counter, wash my hands, and lean back. I inhale sharply when I feel Wesley's hand slide around my waist and his chin come to rest on my shoulder.

"Morning." I rest the side of my head against his.

"Morning, gorgeous." He kisses my neck, and my body relaxes back into his.

This moment is nothing like the last time I was in a bathroom taking a pregnancy test. I have no worries. Not only do Wesley and I have a solid relationship but we got married five months ago—a month after Dustin's first birthday, which made everything with us complete.

"How long do we have to wait?" his sleepy voice rumbles. I turn my head and meet his gaze.

"About three minutes," I say, seeing the anxiousness in his gaze. Then again, he's been anxious every month for the last ten—since we said that we were going to try for another baby.

When the screen finally flashes and the answer we have been waiting for appears, I feel him tense behind me.

"Am I seeing things?"

"No," I whisper as love and happiness overwhelm me.

"Jesus." His hand moves to my stomach, and his face moves to the crook of my neck.

Covering his hand with my own, I close my eyes and soak in this feeling.

"Mama. Dada," Dustin says.

I turn in Wesley's arms to watch Dustin stumble sleepily into the bathroom, rubbing his eyes.

"Hey, baby." I smile at my boy, and he comes over to me and his dad, holding out his arms. Reaching down, I pick him up.

Wesley wraps his arms around the two of us.

"I love you two," he says gruffly.

I swallow over the lump in my throat, then kiss Dustin's chubby cheek.

"I love you both, too," I whisper. Then I laugh, dropping my head to his chest. "Who would have thought being stood up and stumbling into you would turn out to be the best thing that ever happened to me?"

Acknowledgments

First, I have to give thanks to God, because without Him, none of this would be possible. Second, I want to thank my husband. I love you now and always—thank you for believing in me even when I don't believe in myself. My beautiful son, you bring such joy into my life, and I'm so honored to be your mom.

To every blogger and reader, thank you for taking the time to read and share my books. There would never be enough ink in the world to acknowledge you all, but I will forever be grateful to each and every one of you.

I started this writing journey after I fell in love with reading, like thousands of authors before me. I want to give people a place to escape. A place where the stories are funny, sweet, hot, and leave you feeling good. I have loved sharing my stories with you all, loved that I have helped people escape the real world, even for a moment.

I started writing for me, but I will continue writing for you.

XOXO Aurora

About the Author

Aurora Rose Reynolds's writing career started out as an attempt to clear her head of too many outrageously alpha guys. Now, after writing a number of wildly popular series, including Until, Until Him, Until Her, and Underground Kings, Aurora is a *New York Times* and *USA Today* bestselling author. She is also the author of *Running Into Love*, the first book in her flirty romance series Fluke My Life.

Aurora is no stranger to alpha males. Aside from being a navy brat, her husband also served in the navy, and he gives her plenty of that hot alpha love and inspiration every day. They live together in Tennessee. Aurora's fans are invited to follow her on Twitter (@Auroraroser) or connect with her at www.AuroraRoseReynolds.com.